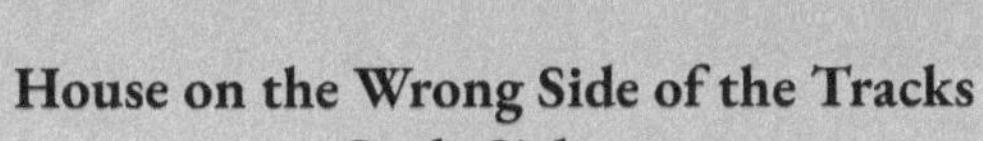

# House on the Wrong Side of the Tracks
## Gayle Siebert

Cover Art Design by: Kelly Moran/Rowan Prose Publishing
Photo Credit: Adobe Images/Deposit Photos
First Edition
ISBN: 978-1-961967-65-6
Rowan Prose Publishing, LLC
www.RowanProsePublishing.com
Published in the United States of America

# DEDICATION

*To all the horses that have been and are in my life.*
*Without them, I wouldn't be who I am.*

# Chapter 1

Alphonse Asselstine is boring. I think I'll slip into a coma if I have to surveil him another minute. All he ever does is sit. In his little office. In his truck. In his living room in front of the TV. If nothing pops today, my assignment ends in failure.

It's my first assignment from Saskatchewan Government Insurance, a real feather in my cap. He claims he's too injured to do physical work so he can't fix up the old house he was planning to flip, which he says was going to make him a bundle. There goes his early retirement. My mission: to catch him at something he claims he can't do. Video of him sitting on his ample backside won't do it. He moves so seldom I wouldn't have had to go into debt to buy the camcorder.

The second day, it looked promising. He went to his project house, took something that might have been a toolbox inside, and—came right back out with it. I got video of him getting in and out of the truck with no sign of a sore back, but no judge would deny his claim based on that. And every time I've followed him, he does the same thing: leaves his job as dispatcher at Swift Taxi, heads to the old house, goes in, and comes back out half an hour later. Sometimes he stays longer, but whatever he's doing in there doesn't make enough noise to be heard outside. With the windows boarded up, I can't even get a look inside.

At home, he ignores overgrown bushes, lawn grass so tall it's going to seed, and weeds crowding the house. He sits by the window drinking beer until his wife calls him for supper. And K.C. wonders why I call him Beer Belly Boy.

Today being Saturday, I thought he'd spend time at the old house, but his truck isn't there. It's not at his domicile either. I decide to wait in case he comes home, so I tuck my van in beside the neighbor's hedge and settle in. I'm in luck. He drives in, and when he gets out from behind the wheel, he's carrying a twenty-four of Lucky. In minutes, I hear football games on TV. The volume is turned to ear-splitting to drown out the hum of the fan on the window ledge. His wife is either deaf or a saint, putting up with that.

The shadows are growing. It seems unlikely he'll do any work around the place this late and I'm about to give up and go home, when he comes out and gets in his pickup. I duck so if he notices my van, he can't see me in it. After giving him a brief head start, I follow. I get caught on the wrong side of a traffic light, and when the light's green again, I've lost him. In hopes of picking him up again, I drive on and soon spot his truck pulling into a parking stall at The Stockmen's. I turn into the lot, drive to the far end, and park. With the Handycam stashed in the console bin, I don my Saskatchewan Roughriders ballcap, pull my ponytail out through the hole in the back, and head for the pub entrance.

The Stockmen's smells like every other pub I've been in: stale beer, cigarette smoke, and beef on the grill, with hints of backed-up sewer. The place is busy, the chatter loud, Garth Brooks on the jukebox bragging about his friends in low places rumbling away in the background. The ballcap was a good idea, because I blend right in.

When my eyes have adjusted to the dim lighting, I spot my target on a stool at the bar. There are a couple of empty seats on that side of the bar, including one right beside him, all useless to me. The only other empty stool is on the end, between two guys. I take it. From here, I can covertly watch him in the mirror behind the bar.

I order a glass of house white. The guys on either side of me seem to think my Roughriders cap is a sign I'm a fan, but all I know about the 'Riders is that they won the Grey Cup last year. The cowboy on my right is yammering about their two wins and two losses so far this season and if he was the coach he'd do this, that, or the other, or else 1990 won't be a repeat. He predicts they'll beat the Edmonton Eskimos on Tuesday since they're coming off a win last week against the B.C. Lions. He looks at me and says, "Right?"

"Um..."

The forty-something guy in the South Saskatchewan Fracking ballcap on my left saves me from answering by disagreeing loudly, and they get into a spirited discussion. I suggest we trade seats so they're not talking over me. They comply.

Another mug of beer is delivered to Beer Belly Boy. It's well past supper time and despite the stench of sewer, my stomach is growling. I'd love to order a Caesar salad, but I'd only have to leave it if that's it for him. I can't sit here nursing a six-ounce glass of wine for long, though, so since he shows no signs of moving, I order another. Damn! Two glasses of wine and I've eaten nothing but a sandwich nine hours ago. I'll be too drunk to drive if he doesn't make a move soon. I suppose I could've ordered a ginger ale, but I tell myself since one of our family businesses is winemaking, it's research. When he orders a third mug of beer, I order the salad.

The bartender asks, "Are you sure you don't want to run a tab?"

"I'm sure."

I didn't need to worry about my target leaving when I was mid-salad, because he orders a fourth mug. Before long, a large, heavily-made-up woman slides onto a stool midway down the bar. She orders a glass of house red. When her wine comes, I hear Beer Belly tell the bartender to put it on his tab. She rewards him with a smile. He moves onto the stool next to her and they strike up a conversation.

When the woman is on her second glass, the two of them begin sucking face with abandon. I wonder how I manage to keep my salad down. It looks like a good time for a comfort break, so I put the coaster on top of my glass and go to the ladies' room. When I'm done there and come back, the two lovebirds are gone. At least I can't see them at a table anywhere. I give the bartender a little wave and when he's in front of me, ask, "Oh, hey, where did the two that were at the other end of the bar move to?" When he gives me a quizzical look, I hurry on: "I just realized she used to be one of my teachers, and I was going to go say hi."

"She's a teacher? Really?"

Does he know her? Is the idea of her being a teacher too far-fetched? But it was all I could come up with at the moment. "I think so," I reply, and add, "I mean, maybe. I could be wrong. It's been a few years."

"Whaddaya know," he says. "Well, you missed 'em by two minutes."

"Thanks," I say, swig the last of my wine, and race out into the dark parking lot hoping to see them pressed up against the wall or a car or something. But there's no one anywhere. His truck is still where he parked it. Damn! They must have left in the woman's car. There's no chance I'll find them now.

Defeated, I head for my van, but as I'm passing behind the guy's truck, I notice movement in the cab. Country music? The windows must be open. They haven't gone after all, but are inside, trading spit like a couple of teenagers.

I race to my van and get my Handycam, then slink into the row of scruffy bushes bordering the parking lot and work my way along until I'm right in front of his truck. I was worried I might be seen, but even though I'm mere feet away, I couldn't have a better blind if I planned it. The nearest overhead light isn't far off and the video camera is pretty good in low light. With luck it'll even pick up the audio.

I snagged my shirt on something and the smell wafting up around me suggests I've got dog shit on my boots, but my main problem is stopping myself from laughing. Things in the cab soon progress to the point that I can't see much of either of them, but there's a foot in a wedge-heeled sandal on the dash. Her moans are loud enough to be heard over the radio. "Oh, baby! You make me so hot! That's it! I'm ready, honey!" And more in that vein. She's not much of an actress. Beer Belly Boy would have to be as dumb as a post to believe she's really into it. But he must be that dumb, because he pops up and into view as he climbs on top. They're both moaning and groaning now. He barely gets a rhythm going before uttering a loud, "Gaaahh!"

She says, "Whatsamatter, baby?"

"My goddamn back!" He straightens up and they have a quiet discussion. They must have concluded things would work better if he were to sit up and have her climb on him, because that's what they do. It's a rather tight fit owing to Beer Belly Boy's beer belly, and to call her pleasantly plump would be a kindness.

It's hard work. She plays out quickly. Apparently it's enough as there's a number of heartfelt *oh gods* and then a loud, lengthy *"Gaaahhh!"* They reposition themselves so they're sitting side by side, and light cigarettes. Clouds of smoke issue from the windows. I imagine they're whispering whatever a john and a hooker whisper at such a time. In a moment, the passenger door opens. She climbs out, straightens her skirt, stuffs her immense breasts back inside her bra, and buttons her blouse. In a voice loud enough to be heard at the other end of the parking lot, she sticks her hand in the window and says, "Next week, Alfie?"

Alfie? She knows his name. He must be a regular. He mumbles a reply, but I can't make out what it is. He hands her something, payment I guess, as she tucks it into her cleavage and walks away.

You'd think I'd be disgusted with myself for being a peeping Lindy, but instead, I'm so pleased at getting this great evidence I feel like dancing.

On Monday, I present myself at the office of Jesse Bird & Co., anxious to impress him with the video. I get my Handycam connected to the TV in the lunchroom, and when Jesse and the other half of Jesse and Company, his wife and secretary Eileen, are ready to watch, turn it on.

I give them a running commentary, but mostly let the video speak for itself. Jesse and Eileen are quiet except for low chuckles that could be surprise or humor or maybe embarrassment. When it's finished, I ask, "What do you think? He's able to move around pretty well, at least until she climbs on."

"I dunno, Lindy," Jesse says. "It kind of confirms his back is injured, and—"

"Yeah, I know," I cut in, "he complains about his back, but it doesn't really slow him down. I was thinking more that he wouldn't want this video to come out. I know it's 1990 and people aren't puritanical these days, but he wouldn't want his wife to see him with a hooker. So maybe it's enough to get him to go away?"

"Only one problem. She's Mrs. Asselstine."

"What? She's his wife?"

"Yeah. What you have on video is date night, I guess."

I ponder this news, then ask, "Even so, romping like that in the cab of a truck? Isn't that enough to prove he's faking?"

"Maybe, if we hadn't heard him complain about his back."

When no one speaks for what seems like an hour, I ask, "Can I still submit my bar bill for reimbursement?"

I've finished payroll as well as issuing checks for suppliers, when K.C. comes in, Saran-wrapped plate in hand. "Red sent you a sandwich," he says, and sets it on my desk. "Chicken salad."

"Thanks. I'm finished here, so I don't have to eat at my desk," I tell him. "I'll join you at the island."

"I already ate. Cream of mushroom soup today."

"Kind of a hot day for soup, isn't it?"

"Maybe, but it's my favorite."

"Yeah, I know," I reply. I get up to give him a kiss, but he's already turned away. I pick up the plate and follow him out into the kitchen. "You get all your horses rode already?"

"Pretty much," he replies. He gets a mug of the coffee I made about two hours ago, but instead of taking a seat at the island with me, he leans his skinny butt back against the counter.

"That's a short session today, then."

"Didn't ride that big colt. You know, the one the kids named Rocky?" At my nod, he continues, "Worked him pretty hard yesterday, and with him being so big already and still growing, I figured he could use the time off."

"You still like him?"

"Yeah, even though he's got that spook and buck like I told you. No small thing, not with a big moving horse like him.

Besides that, he's been so pissy lately you'd think he was a mare. I wish he'd get over his bad mood and start acting like a gelding."

I nearly say what I'm thinking, that I know someone else who's been acting like a mare and judging by the current state of our sex life, might as well be a gelding. Instead I say, "Too big, too much movement, and too much attitude."

"Yup, that's him. Plus, he's got a big trot, something else no cowboy's looking for. His canter's going to be great once he gets more balanced, though. Not the makings of a cowhorse, but he'll be a decent dressage prospect. Got some draft in him. Came from a PMU farm, I'd guess."

I click my tongue and say, "It's so sad. All those babies shipped for meat, just to get the pregnant mare urine."

"But you don't want to give up your birth control pills, do you?" he asks. His tone is harsh, and he frowns at me before turning away to gaze out the window over the sink.

I remind myself that I love him, so instead of snapping back, I reply in an even tone, "No, but it's 1990, not 1960. You'd think they'd've found something better by now. Besides, people should be married if they want to have kids."

The Pill and getting married—both touchy subjects. I had hoped our heated discussion at breakfast put an end to it. I don't see how a baby would fit into my life. I'm too busy, what with running the ranch I inherited and starting my private investigator business. Sure, the Lindy Larsen, P.I. phone isn't ringing off the hook and has never needed its maximum ten message storage capacity, but that may change, and when I'm on assignment I can be away from home for hours on end. If I'm honest with myself, though, I have to admit I just don't have the necessary maternal instinct.

"You know my ex won't give me a divorce. Besides, a marriage licence is just ink on paper. The important thing is to be in a committed relationship," he says, bringing my thoughts back into our conversation.

The way things have been going for the past months, I'm not sure how committed our relationship actually is. I ignore his comment about marriage licences. On the subject of birth control, though, I say, "I still say they should be able to synthesize something, so they don't need the PMU."

"Um hmm." He drains his coffee and sets his mug on the counter above the dishwasher before turning and starting toward the door.

I ask, "You busy this afternoon?"

He holds up in the doorway and replies, "As always. Why?"

"Well, if you don't have anything pressing, I need to take mail to the post office. And I thought since I'm done early and have extra time, maybe I'd take a run into Swift Current to check out that new tack shop."

"Oh yeah? You need something you can't get at the tack shop right in town?"

"I need a new shirt for the rodeo. Too much time on my butt, what with office work and hours in my van. Hasn't done my waistline any good. I've put on a few pounds, so my jeans are uncomfortably tight, and I don't have a shirt with snaps that stay shut. I've already seen the ones at the Hitching Post, and I don't like any of them."

He fusses with the loose weatherstripping on the doorjamb, but says nothing.

To sweeten the pot, I add, "We could go for dinner at Pioneer House."

"Okay. When're you leaving?"

"Whenever you're ready."

"Give me half an hour," he says.

Would he have agreed to go if I hadn't suggested dinner at his favorite restaurant? I doubt it. Sadness at the current state of our relationship squeezes my insides. I've been told many times that whatever I'm feeling shows on my face, so I turn away.

# Chapter 2

I mail the checks and buy a booklet of stamps at the post office, then with K.C. behind the wheel, we head north. It takes about an hour to drive from Maple Creek to Swift Current. I wouldn't say the mood in the cab is chilly, exactly, but we're a long way from *can't keep our hands off each other* that was us not long ago.

The cooling off started when K.C. first mentioned wanting a kid. I pointed out that he has two from his first marriage, and maybe it's time they started visiting the ranch. They could spend weeks here during school holidays. Wouldn't that be enough? No, because they're *his and hers*, not *his and mine*. Besides, his ex would never allow it. Why? A list of issues including, oddly enough, both kids having asthma, and her fear the horses would hurt them. Seems like she also has a hate on for me even though I'm not the reason he left her, and we've never met. I told him I thought the courts would enforce his visitation rights and he could bring them to the ranch whether she liked it or not. And as for our own kid, that was definitely something we should've talked about before he moved in, and if he was serious about it, he should've done whatever it took to get a divorce. That's how we left it. Unresolved and festering.

At Creekside Tack, I pick out jeans a size larger than my usual and find a shirt I love on the markdown rack, also in my new size. Dieting is looking like something I should quit putting off.

K.C. can't find anything he wants. Once back in the truck, says, "That was a bust. We might as well have saved a tank of gas and gone to the Hitchin' Post."

I don't point out that I already told him I couldn't find anything I liked in Maple Creek, it doesn't take a tank of gas to go to Swift Current, and Maple Creek doesn't have a Pioneer House Restaurant. He knows those things.

The food at the Pioneer House is great, as usual. Besides operating a winery, we raise cattle, so we get plenty of beef at home—roasted, chicken-fried, stewed, barbequed, meatloaf-ed and hamburger-ed, you name it—but we don't raise pigs, and K.C. loves the baby back ribs. I always opt for the grilled whitefish.

We talk about his upcoming clinic in Saskatoon. He says it's full and they might add a day. I tell him we need a new microwave in the Bistro. The one I brought with me when I moved to the ranch was never intended for use in a commercial kitchen. The lower interlock switch has shorted out and been fixed three times now. He asks how much it would cost to replace, and when I tell him, he says, "It's been fixed before, and it can be fixed again. Wait until it craps out for good." His tone suggests that ends the discussion. I could tell him that just because I don't argue doesn't mean I agree, and it's not his decision. It's been budgeted for, and I've already ordered another one. I don't tell him that, either.

I ask myself when we last laughed together. It used to happen every day and now that seems like a lifetime ago. Having a conversation with him is really getting to be hard work. At least there is no further mention of me and The Pill.

As we're walking out, K.C. reaches for my hand. I'm surprised and pleased. So much so that I nearly abandon my plan. Nearly, but not quite. When we get to the truck, I say, "I'll drive." He looks perplexed. "You drove here, after all," I explain, and give him what I hope is a winning smile as I release his hand and go to the driver's door. He shrugs and goes around to the passenger side.

Pioneer House is in a neighborhood a realtor would describe as improving, wedged between the railroad tracks and the Trans Canada Highway.

"Wrong turn, babe," K.C. says, as when we're leaving, I turn left and cross the tracks into an area that looks like a ghost town. The stench of the nearby stockyards permeates everything. This is what the term *wrong side of the tracks* was coined for. I call it Dogpatch.

"Um, well…" I ignore his sigh and continue, "So, remember that guy I was surveilling a few weeks ago? Well, that old house he was supposedly fixing up is just a couple blocks out of our way."

"And we care why?"

"I'm just interested, that's all. I thought since I've talked about it so much, maybe you'd like to see it."

"I wouldn't, but since you didn't ask me, we're going to do what you want."

So much for K.C. mellowing out. He probably won't hold my hand again for a while. I could argue there are plenty of his ideas I go along with even though I don't agree, but decide against it, and say nothing. In fairness, I knew he'd say no if I asked, but I really wanted to take a look since we were this close. I drive on.

On a cross street at the edge of the bald open prairie, I slow and point to the house. Its windows are covered with plywood, there's a large, conspicuous padlock on the door and *No Tres-*

*passing* signs are plastered everywhere. With no near neighbors, just a swath of open grassland on one side and on the other, the concrete foundation of a house long since demolished, it's about as remote an urban location as you could find. The three run-down houses we come to next look as if they were built about the same time and by the same builder. No one has bothered to board up the broken windows.

"Those faded signs on the doors? These houses are all condemned," I say.

"Look like a bunch of Sears kit houses," K.C. says.

"Kit houses?"

"Yeah. Used to be you could order a house from the Sears catalogue and they'd ship it to you. The original prefab house."

"Really? I never heard of that before. That's one of the things I like about you, you know so much stuff," I tell him. I sound like such a suck up I almost gag on the words. I thought he'd appreciate the ego stroking, but his only response is a shrug, as if to say *well, duh!*

The street ends at the edge of a ravine. I turn left and then left again to go up the back lane. Caragana hedges on both sides are so overgrown that in places, the lane is nearly blocked. Grass and weeds, going to seed, grow tall everywhere. Clouds of grasshoppers take to the air as we approach.

"I wonder why the houses are all condemned. They don't look any worse than the one Beer Belly Boy is renovating, other than the windows on his house are boarded up."

"I'm sure his is condemned, too. It just means they don't have water and sewer," K.C. says, and points. "Outhouses. If your guy thinks he's going to retire on the money he makes by renovating and flipping that thing, I hope he got it for a song, or he'll lose his shirt. He'd have to connect to water and sewer first and that ain't cheap."

"Maybe he thinks when a developer buys the rest of these shacks, he'll be the lone holdout and make money without doing anything." I pull to a stop behind Beer Belly Boy's project house. "It sure doesn't look like anything's been done since I was last here."

"Did it occur to you maybe that's because he can't work, just like he claims? If he could, he'd at least have the power hooked up. It's cut off at the pole," he says, and points.

I look up at the utility pole he's pointing at realize there is no power line to the house. What renovating can he be doing that doesn't require power?

"Let's get going, Lindy," K.C. says, breaking into my thoughts. "Lots of things I'd rather be doing than poking around this rat hole."

*Rat hole* is what my ex called the ranch I inherited, so K.C. coming out with that term stings, even without his sharp tone. Wacasko-Wâti is the Cree equivalent, more or less, of rat hole. I named the ranch Wacasko-Wâti to thumb my nose at my ex as well as to acknowledge that it's in the ancestral lands of the Nekaneet Cree. I grin and think, *take that, Charles Bailey!*

"Something funny?" K.C. asks.

"No, well, I was just—"

He waves a hand in my direction and clicks his tongue.

I don't finish my thought and instead retreat into my mind. Why do I care about a closed file? Call me a poor loser, but I don't want Beer Belly Boy to get a dime for his fake injury. I couldn't catch him in a lie, so I got nothing of value for the insurance company. An unimpressive first assignment. If they haven't settled his claim yet, it might not be too late to prove he's malingering. It would shine up my reputation. If my P.I. business was doing better, maybe K.C. wouldn't resent the payments on my van and Camcorder as much as he does. Snooping into people's lives is the private investigator's job description.

Thanks to my suspicious nature, it suits me perfectly. Also, although I probably shouldn't be proud of it, I'm a gifted liar. Good reasons for loving the job. Love the job, sure, but I'd be a lot happier if K.C. was on board.

If I thought looking at the project house would stimulate K.C.'s interest in my new career, it was a *beer belly* flop. I try to recall what's on my calendar for the next week or think of an excuse to come back to Swift Current.

The footpath to the outhouse is used enough that it's clear of weeds. That's not surprising, because Beer Belly Boy would need it. What is curious, though, is something else I didn't notice before: a hasp and padlock on the man door into the dilapidated garage beside it. My curiosity shifts into overdrive. What could warrant locking that up? But K.C.'s not interested, so if I want to know, I'll have to come back another time. With my lock pick set and without him.

This time my grin is only in my mind.

Beer Belly Boy wasn't my only file so far, just the most interesting. Straying husbands and cheating wives don't exactly keep me run off my feet, but at least they pay a few bills. And happy day! I get a new assignment from Saskatchewan Government Insurance. This means that despite not getting them anything they could use to deny his claim, they liked my work on the file enough to hire me again.

Today I finish my office work early enough to take the deposit to the bank before the three o'clock closing time, so I won't have to use the night deposit. As I'm coming out of the bank, I see a familiar truck going by in the street. Beer Belly Boy? What's a taxi dispatcher from Swift Current doing so far from home on a workday? Minutes later as I'm driving home, I almost miss seeing his truck in the drive-through at Tim Horton's. Whatever he's doing here, he's not in a hurry to leave. Or maybe he's been somewhere else, needed a break, and decided to swing into Maple Creek. But Maple Creek isn't exactly on the way to anywhere. I pull over to the curb and wait for him to leave. Although I wait half an hour, I don't see him again. Would he use the drive-through to buy something and then park in the lot to eat it? When traffic clears, I make a U-turn, cruise slowly past Tim Horton's, and confirm his truck isn't there. He must have turned the other way instead of heading back to Swift Current. I don't know what I thought I was going to do, anyway. Follow him? Maybe K.C.'s right and I should quit obsessing. I head home.

When I drive in, I'm surprised to see K.C. coming out of the barn. He was supposed to be delivering horses to Calgary today and should have left before now. He's coming my way, his frown obvious even at this distance. I'm barely out of the truck when he demands, "Where've you been?"

"In town. You knew I—"

"You should've been home an hour ago."

I can't think of a believable lie, so I tell him the truth. "I spotted Beer Belly Boy's truck and wondered, what's he doing here? When I surveilled him, he never left Swift Current—"

"Don't tell me you followed him."

"Well, I thought I might, but—"

"Jesus, Lindy, give your head a shake! Why?"

"Well, obviously I thought I had a good reason. Let's just leave it at that. And anyway, I finished everything I had to do here, so what's the big frickin' deal?'

"We need your truck. You knew we had to deliver those horses to Calgary today. We need both trailers."

"Yeah? So?"

"Stu's truck has chosen today to break down, so we need yours."

"How is that my fault?"

His frown is intense, and I have the fleeting thought that if he was a dog, I wouldn't make eye contact. "That's not your fault, obviously, but if you hadn't been pissing around with that Beer Belly Boy nonsense, you'd've been here and we wouldn't be an hour behind schedule. We're supposed to meet the new owners at six, which obviously we won't now, and we'll be lucky to be home by midnight."

"Don't lay this on me. You didn't have to sell your four-horse trailer," I say.

"Actually, I did. Where'd you think the money for the wash rack in my indoor came from?" He holds out his hand and demands, "Keys?"

I clamp my teeth together, drop my keys in his hand and ask, "What, no kiss hello?"

He's already past me but I didn't really want a kiss anyway, because with him snarling at me like he did, I'm afraid he might bite. You'd think he'd be in a good mood, having sold those horses, but instead, he's someone I barely recognize.

Cattle prices are still poor, but the winery, farm store and Bistro are doing okay. Not a single additional Cameron Larsen love child has shown up claiming a share of my inheritance. K.C. has sold enough horse trailers, has enough horses in training, and has booked enough clinics that he has cash in his jeans for the foreseeable future. Life at Wacasko-Wâti rolls along.

I've just finished a report for SGI. There are a dozen colour photos and a video to go with it. The cassette is bulky and heavy, not something I can just put in an envelope and guess at how many stamps are needed, so I have to take it to the post office. The claims examiner has already phoned to ask about it, so I want to get to the post office in time for the last mail pick up. Also—important detail—my invoice is with it. I trot out to my truck and I'm just about to leave the parking lot when a strikingly handsome cowboy appears at my window. "Got a couple minutes, Auntie? I really need to talk to you."

Felix is the nephew of my best friend, business partner, and Stu's wife, Red. I'm not actually a relative, but I like that he calls me Auntie. He's one of my favourite people and I hate to put him off. I glance at my watch, and explain, "I'm running out of time to get this to the post office before it closes. Can it wait until I get back?"

"It's important," he assures me.

"Okay. Hop in. You can tell me all about it on the way into town."

"Okay, sure," he says, and trots around to the passenger side.

Once we're heading down the road, I say, "Okay, Felix, what is it that's so important?"

"You know my friend Joe?"

Joe is one of our seasonal field workers. "Sure. Why?"

"It's not about him, really," Felix replies. "It's his cousin Wesley."

"Wesley?" I wrack my brain but can't remember the name or come up with a face. "Should I know who that is?"

"No. He's never worked for you, and he doesn't live on the Rez. He lives in Regina. It's not about him, exactly. You remember hearing about the missing girl?"

"Um, yeah. That was a while ago, right? Haven't heard much lately."

"That's right, and that's the problem. It's been a month, and we don't hear anything about it. Anyhow, her name is Janey. She's Wesley's daughter."

"Oh no! That's terrible! But that's a police matter, right? Nothing I can do, right?"

"Well, maybe. That is, maybe there is more you can do. I'll help too, because the thing is, the cops keep saying a missing person is a top priority for them and they're doing all they can, but they ain't doing a damn thing."

"Maybe it doesn't look like it, but I'm sure they are. They're not going to tell me anything they aren't telling Wesley." I glance at him, just long enough to see the tension in his face. He knows as well as I do someone missing that long is unlikely to be found alive. In a softer tone I say, "Is it possible she ran away?"

"No, Janey would never do that. She's the most responsible kid you could imagine."

"But you know, Regina is a three hour drive. A little more, actually. How am I—I mean how are *we*—going to do any investigating when we're looking at six plus hours of just travel time?"

"Oh, I should've said, she doesn't live with Wes. Him and his wife split, and Janey lives with her mom in Webb."

"Webb... That whistlestop just west of Swift Current?"

"That's it. She's only fifteen, but she had a job at the Dairy Queen in Swift Current. She goes there after school and then gets a ride home with Dee. That's her mom. Last time anyone seen her, she left work and was on her way to the Husky truck stop where Dee works."

"Hitchhiking?"

"No. She walks to the Husky and waits inside or goes sleep in Dee's car until Dee gets off."

"Hmm."

As if sensing my doubts she would pass up a ride if offered, Felix reiterates, "She knows better than to take a ride."

We ride along in silence for a few minutes. At last I ask, "What do the cops think?"

"They said not to worry, girls her age come home on their own as soon as they run outta money. Wesley flipped out, punched a cop, and wound up in jail." Felix shakes his head slowly and drops his chin to his chest as he examines the floor between his boots. "Didn't do his cause any good. I don't blame him, though. I might do the same thing if it was me."

"Yeah. Well." Thoughts spin through my head. We're unlikely to be successful, but at least Felix would feel like he was doing something. "How about this. You go talk to Wesley. Find out everything you can about Janey. She might have friends in Regina, you know, that she made when she visited him. Get their names and contact info. See if you can run them down and interview them. But before that, see if Dee has a current photo. Find out about her friends in Webb and Swift Current. She might not have a boyfriend, but she must have other school friends. We need to make posters and get them put up everywhere. It's going to be time consuming and there'll be a cost for gas. Copies aren't cheap either. You prepared for that?"

I glance across at him. His lips are pressed firmly together and a muscle in his jaw works as he nods.

# Chapter 3

It's Marcie's day off, so I'm manning the tasting bar in the wine room. The patio doors are open, and Felix is outside, surrounded by a dozen people. He's handing out posters he picked up from Kwick Kopy this morning.

Dwight is prominent in the group. He was NCO in Charge of Maple Creek RCMP Detachment, but he retired last fall. I think he's finding himself at loose ends, because he's been hanging around Wacasko-Wâti, visiting his buddy Stu and even pitching in to help with such shit jobs as cleaning bulk feed bins or wine vats just for something to do. He says it's to repay us for all the free cinnamon buns and coffee over the years, but I think he's bored. There's only so much puttering to be done around a city lot and there's always plenty of work here. Also, I think he's taking the opportunity to get away from his wife. If that's it, I'm surprised it took this long, because I'd seen enough of that the first night I met her. Funny how things change. When they first got together not that long ago, we never saw him without Theresa. He seemed pretty stoked that she stuck to him like a burr on your sock. Maybe it's a reminder that relationships evolve, and K.C.'s and mine cooling off is just the way of things.

When the volunteers all have their posters and leave, I expect Dwight and Felix to come in so we can chat for a bit. Instead, they follow the others. There are no customers in the wine bar, so I go to the door to tell them where I am. But there's an RCMP cruiser I hadn't seen drive in parked at the curb, and Gerard, one of the new constables, is standing in the open door. Dwight and Felix hold up beside him.

I'm curious, but decide against horning in on their conversation. Gerard comes in for coffee and a cinnamon bun often, too, so I expect it's idle cop chitchat, and they'll come to update me. But when Gerard gets back in his cruiser and drives away, Felix and Dwight head across the parking lot to the picnic table on my private patio.

I go to the kitchen and call out, "Hey, guys! If I'm needed in the tasting room, give me a shout, will you? I'll be over on my patio." I leave without waiting for a reply and hurry across the parking lot to join the two men. I stop short when I see Felix's expression. I've seen him hobbling around on a smashed ankle after being stomped by a bull he was bucked off of, but I've never seen him struggling not to cry.

"What is it?" I ask.

Dwight turns to me with a look that almost matches Felix's and says, "She's been found, Lindy."

The mood around my patio tonight is somber. Felix has gone to meet Wesley at Dee's. Dwight still hasn't gone home. If he hadn't retired, he might be giving us the inside scoop on Janey's murder, but now he doesn't know more than we do. He, Red and Stu are opposite K.C. and me at the picnic table. Charlie and Johnny are looking after night feed and the Bistro is closed, so we adults are off duty now.

We've asked the same question over and over: who would do such a thing?

I say, "I wouldn't be surprised if Janey wasn't his first kill."

"Why would you think that?" Dwight asks.

"Because she's got a wild imagination," K.C. says before I can answer. "Finding out her old buddy Russ Benson was a serial killer makes her suspicious of everyone."

"I wish you'd quit calling Russ my old buddy. He was old rodeo pal of Stu's and my dad's," I remind him. "Second, she's not the first girl to turn up dead. Last fall, there was that woman in Medicine Hat."

"She was a prostitute and a drug addict. Risky lifestyle and a soft target," Dwight tells us.

"Not to mention Medicine Hat is more than a hundred miles from Swift Current," K.C. points out.

"So what? Two hour drive at most." I can't stop myself from giving K.C. a sharp look. "It's not like he'd have to walk, for God's sake. And there's some pretty sketchy characters right in this neck of the woods. Like the guy I was surveilling in Swift Current—"

"Oh, my God," K.C. exclaims, "don't start in on that!"

"What's that about, Lindy?" Dwight asks.

Thank you, Dwight! He knows from past experience that my suspicions shouldn't be discounted. "It's a guy I call Beer Belly Boy, for obvious reasons. He's got a shack he claims to be fixing up to sell, but he doesn't even have the electricity hooked up. How do you run power tools without electricity?"

"Generator, maybe?" K.C. says.

"Generator!? That's ridiculous—"

"If only we got on it sooner," Red interrupts loudly. Her glare is a warning for me to cool it before it becomes another argument.

Dwight loops an arm around Red's shoulders. She's so much smaller than he is that she nearly disappears into his armpit when he gives her a squeeze. "He likely killed her within a few days of grabbing her," he says. "Maybe even the same day."

"Where's she been all this time, then?" Red asks.

"Maybe right where she was found. You go down into the badlands. You know how rough and wild it is. What with no access except by guided tours which don't take anyone off the trails, a body could be there for years without being found."

"Well, we go in the back door so we're never with a guided tour. Same could be true for the killer," I point out. "If she was there a month, there would be predation. And decomp—"

"Jesus, Lindy!" K.C. says.

"I'm just saying, I'd feel better if he didn't hold her captive for a month. If he was going to kill her anyway, it would be better if he did it right away. They must be able to tell how long she's been dead," I say. "Can you find out, Dwight?"

"Maybe," he replies. "I'll drop in on the Detachment tomorrow. I should at least be able to find out what they're going to tell the media, ahead of the press release."

"And nobody seen nothing," Stu observes for about the third time. "I don't get it."

"Well, it was dark," Dwight points out.

"But she'd of been walking on a busy road. Both them places are right on the Trans Canada Highway. Surely someone would've seen a scuffle."

"She might've gone with him voluntarily," Dwight suggests.

"So, it could have been someone she knew?" I ask.

"Maybe someone she recognized as a customer," Dwight replies.

"I just hope they catch the guy," I say. "I hope you can find out something, Dwight, and keep us posted."

"Well, sure, as far as I can. And you know, Felix has applied to be a auxiliary cop. He'll keep on top of it."

Red pulls herself out of Dwight's armpit, looks up at him and says, "He wants to be a cop? I'll be go to hell, that's the first I heard of that."

"Could be he wanted to wait until it was a done deal," Dwight says. "Hope I didn't let the cat out of the bag. But I'm sure he'll get in. In fact, they'd love to have him. If Nekaneet was big enough to have its own tribal police force, they'd take him in a heartbeat. Auxiliary is the next best thing. He's exactly what community policing needs. I bet he'll be stationed right here."

"Well, that's great!" I exclaim.

"Just don't let on I told you," Dwight says.

"I wisht he'd of told us," Stu says. "I wonder how he's going to work around his shifts in the winery. We prob'ly need to hire another winemaker. But anyway, we won't say nothing until he brings it up."

"You better not," Dwight warns. Then he grins and gets to his feet. "Well, I'll be heading out. Good night, everyone."

We all respond with our good-byes. He heads to his truck and is gone.

"Huh, whaddaya know," I say, "Felix, a cop? He has girls all over him now and he's just a rodeo champion. Can you imagine what he'll look like in a uniform? He'll have to beat them off with a stick."

"That's what I'd call a quality problem," K.C. says.

I know I shouldn't read anything into that comment, but I can't help wondering if K.C. wishes he had that problem. And then I realize maybe he does. I know there were always flocks of women around him at his barn in Katawasis Lake, and come to think of it, there are probably three women for every man on his student list.

A knot of dread settles in my stomach. I wonder if he's still fending them off. Is he cheating on me? Is that why he hardly ever wants sex anymore? And the way I've been feeling toward him lately, do I care?

I'm hanging around Jesse's office in no hurry to return home, both because the Bistro is closed Mondays so there's no chance I'll be needed there, and because it's nice to be away from K.C. Sure never thought I'd feel this way. I claimed I needed office supplies and escaped into town. I guess I should go buy paperclips or something before I go home.

Jesse's practice is never super busy and there are no clients in the office now, so we're drinking coffee and generally chit-chatting about a file I'm working on for him while we peoplewatch. His office was formerly a Red & White store. Our chairs in the waiting area give a view out the store front windows. The bank I used to work at and the South Saskatchewan Fracking company offices are across the street, and being on the main drag through town, there's a steady stream of vehicles and pedestrians. Mostly it's just background activity, nothing remarkable, although I point out a South Saskatchewan Fracking truck pulling in to park in front of their office.

"Have you guys noticed all the oil company trucks around lately?"

"No more than usual," Jesse says.

"You don't think so? I don't think I've ever seen so many."

"Well, there's always lots here coming and going from their office, and you know, last I heard there were about two hundred working wells around here. We're in the Bakken Oil Shale Basin, after all. Bound to be plenty of oil company trucks around."

"Hmm. That many wells, eh? In the what? Bakken what?"

"A geological area. Shale rock that has oil trapped in it. It's not just here, it extends all the way from Alberta into Montana and North Dakota."

"I know there's been talk about oil for as long as I've been living here, but I had no idea it had progressed that far."

"Yup, Saskatchewan's going to be a rich province just like Oilberta," he says.

"That's what I like about you, Jesse, you know stuff. But I don't think I'm imagining it. We've all noticed increased traffic on our road. I've seen so many SSF trucks I think I could draw their logo in my sleep."

"Speaking of trucks with logos," Jesse says, and points at a vehicle in the process of pulling into a parking space across the street. "Did Russ Benson sell his?"

"Not that I know of," I reply. Not the SSF logo, but one even more familiar: Rocking R. That's surprising, because it's been mothballed since Russ got sent up. When I see who climbs out from behind the wheel, my guts churn. What is she doing here? I have a moment's indecision—should I go and talk to her, or ignore her and wait until she comes to Wacasko-Wâti in hopes that she doesn't? But that's a faint hope. I jump to my feet and head for the door, saying, "Thanks for coffee. See you."

I check for traffic and trot across the street, behind the truck and onto the sidewalk.

"Trina?" I say.

She's getting something out of the passenger seat and turns to face me. If I was surprised to see my half-sister, I'm rendered speechless when I see what she's holding.

She doesn't seem surprised to see me, though. She just grins and says, "Oh, hey, *sister*. Meet your new nephew."

# Chapter 4

I t's after eight and the day is finally cooling down. We're gathered on the deck at Stu and Red's trailer. Baby Newton is squirming and cooing on Red's lap and Trina is holding court, showing off her diamond ring and gloating about being the owner of the Rocking R.

I can't stop myself from saying, "Well, Trina, you do know Stu owns sixty percent."

"Yeah, but *my husband* already said he'd buy him out, right?

"Sure, and we said no. He also offered to buy Wacasko-Wâti. We're not selling that, either."

"He didn't want it anyway. He just thought he'd buy it for me, because he knows how strong my bond with this land is. A blood bond."

"Blood bond?"

"Don't play dumb," Trina says with a sneer. "I'm as much a part of this place as you are. But Russ figured you wouldn't have the decency to sell it to him."

"It was a shithouse offer, Trina. No way I'd sell for pennies on the dollar," I say.

"Just wait. You will," Trina says, then quickly adds, "anyhow, my forty percent of the Rocking R would be everything from the house to the north property line. I'm going to put up a fence so there's no, um, *confusion*. And I'll thank all of you to stay off it."

"It's not subdivided, Trina. There's no separate title, so we all have the right to go anywhere. If, God forbid, something were to happen to Stu, his share wouldn't go to you. It would go to his wife and kids. So you would find yourself partners with Red and the boys." I tell her this in case she and Russ don't know the difference between tenants in common and joint tenants and are thinking of hastening Stu's demise. A lifer in the Kingston Pen, Russ himself couldn't murder Stu, but someone on the outside might owe him a favor. I give Stu a pointed look in hopes he'll chime in, but he's just nursing his beer and looking like he's slipped into neutral, something I've seen more often lately.

"No way," Trina says.

"Take your title docs to your lawyer if you don't believe me."

She lifts her chin and retorts, "Well, I *don't* believe you. I'll just do that."

"You know you ain't going to live there for free, do you?" Red asks.

"The ranch makes money. We seen how much. Why would I have to pay anything? *You* should be paying *me*," Trina says.

"Well, we ain't going to keep paying all the bills," Red says.

"You've seen how much money the Rocking R *generates*," I say. "That's different than how much it *makes*. By the time you deduct operating costs, there's not a lot of profit," I remind everyone. "And since you say you're going to ship all your cattle, soon you will have no income at all."

"What about the semen? The frozen semen? I mean, why can't it continue the way it is?"

"Once the semen from the last of your bulls sells, you're done. And our guys look after that for nothing. When they start drawing pay, it'll wipe out what little profit it's been making." I give Stu another frown.

He finally sits up and takes notice. He says, "We got a lot of expenses…"

That's where his thoughts seem to trail off, so I add, "We've been picking up all the bills, just as if it was ours. With Russ gone, we had to hire drivers. The trucks need maintenance, and for that matter, so do the buildings. Then there's vets. Farriers. Feed. Tons of other costs. Unless you can drive a bull hauler, have suddenly learned how to work bulls and are strong enough to hump hay bales, you won't be able to contribute what Russ did. How are you going to pay your share?"

"I'll hire someone, same as you," Trina says, and thrusts out her chin. "His share will more than cover it."

"We'll see," I say, and shrug. "Maybe not so much once the free labor isn't free anymore."

Stu didn't feel right being paid for what we'd been doing all along, which was just what every rancher does without thinking. With Russ on the road so much, our guys always did the lion's share of the work anyway, and it's true that having the two sections of Rocking R grazing land to run Wacasko-Wâti's cattle and horses on is a benefit to us. Russ will die in jail. We've talked about who he might leave his share to. I thought Stu, but he's older and might be expected to predecease Russ. After that, who? Red, maybe? They'd been friends for decades. Trina lived with him on the Rocking R for a few months, but when she went back to live with her adoptive parents after Russ got sent up, we thought that was the end of their relationship. It was a shock to learn it had not only continued, but was serious enough that she moved to Ontario to be near the jail. A serial killer, decades older and in jail for life—how could she be stupid enough to marry him, much less have a baby with him?

"Well, besides that, I can come back to work in the Bistro," Trina continues.

I grimace. She was the most useless employee we ever had. I'd like to tell her that we won't take her back, but one look at Red's expression and I realize she's considering it. So, I say, "Who's going to look after your baby while you're working? Day care isn't cheap even if there was such a thing around here."

"I'll bring it with me."

"Absolutely not!" I exclaim. It's not really my decision to make, but Red doesn't argue. I take that as consensus.

"You always hated me because Russ picked me instead of you," Trina snarls. "Right? You're jealous."

"Don't be ridiculous."

"Don't try and deny it. When K.C. was away, you were always coming on to him. Hear that, K.C.? Me and Russ seen right through you, Lindy."

I don't have a chance to respond before Trina adds, "You, *and* the rest of you assholes, you all think you're so much better than everyone else. When I get through with you, you'll *beg* me to buy Wacasko-Wâti!" She jumps to her feet and wrenches her baby out of Red's arms so abruptly he cries out. He's still howling when she scurries down off the deck to her truck and dumps him into the car seat. I'm not sure she even buckles him in before going around to get behind the wheel. She drives away, spewing gravel in a cloud of dust.

"Someone's sure got a low opinion of you, babe," K.C. observes.

Red says, "That baby shouldn't ought to be jerked around like that."

"No, he shouldn't be," I agree. "And she thinks Russ offered to buy Wacasko-Wâti for her because she dreamed up a connection to the land?"

"That's just bullshit," Stu opines, and takes Red's hand. "She never gave a thought 'bout the land until she found out she might be able to get her hands on it. Just too damn bad K.C.

seen her hitchhiking and picked her up. Otherwise she'd never of known…"

His thoughts trail off. I'm not sure if it's another senior's moment or if he didn't want to remind everyone about the secret Red had kept for decades: she and my father had a love child.

"It was never about the land," I agree. "And in case anyone thinks I came on to Russ, I *damn* sure never did. If anything, it was the other way around. Russ flirted with every woman he got near," I say. "You all know that, right?"

"Course we do," Red agrees.

K.C. looks skeptical despite Red's endorsement, so I say, "Kevin Connor Garland! You know that, right?"

"Course I do," he agrees, but the look on his face isn't reassuring. He stretches and stifles a yawn. "On that note, good night, folks." He gets up and starts off without looking my way again.

"I'll come with you," I say, and quickly stand, say good night, and follow. I catch up to him and take his hand as we walk along the path to the end of Red's vegetable garden and through the cottonwood grove to the house. Once inside, I say, "K.C., what's up? We should talk."

"What for? We're good." He heads down the hall to the bathroom and I hear the door close. In moments, the shower starts.

I try the door, but it's locked. I could easily unlock it, and he knows it. But since he's made it obvious he doesn't want me to join him, I decide against it.

We're good? He let me take his hand, but we're a long way from being good.

I won't forget Trina and her threat anytime soon, but after a few days, at least it's not front of mind. K.C. admitted he knows I never tried to seduce Russ, and his mood in general has improved. Maybe it's because of how well his project horses are coming along, or maybe it's because his kids are going to spend a weekend here at Thanksgiving, although he seems a little apprehensive about that. I don't know why he should be. Is he worried his ex won't like where he lives? She balked at the three-hour drive. He removed that roadblock by agreeing to do the driving himself, but I suggested she should make the trip one way at least. That way, she can see for herself that there are no dirt floors and we have indoor plumbing. I guess we'll see how that goes.

I have another assignment from SGI, this time to take a witness statement near Swift Current. One evening I give myself lead time, and with my lock pick set in my van's glove compartment, I swing by Beer Belly Boy's project house, only to find his truck parked at the front steps. I've never known him to be here this late in the day. But then, I did see him in Maple Creek when he would normally be at work. It's a reminder his schedule is variable, and I'll need to be more cautious.

It's damned inconvenient. Now I not only can't break into the shed, but I have an hour to kill before my appointment and nothing to do. I negotiate a three-point turn to go back the way I came, when suddenly, Beer Belly Boy is right in front of me. I'm struck with the realization that he's not bad looking, and he's thinner than I remembered.

I shift into park and roll down the window as he comes up beside me, bringing with him a cloud of smoker's breath. Before he can say anything, I say, "Hi there! Can you tell me how to get to the K Motel?"

He frowns. I've never been this close to him before, and I wish I wasn't so close now. Does he recognize my van from when I was actively surveilling him? I thought I was being super careful, but maybe even an inconspicuous gray van can look out of place. Maintaining eye contact is uncomfortable, but looking away is a sure sign someone's lying. After a moment, he hawks a loogie into the dirt, and says, "No motels out here." He clamps his big fist on the handle as if he might wrench the door open and drag me out.

"Darn it! I'm new in town so I don't know Swift Current that well. I'm supposed to be meeting my friend in the coffee shop. She gave me directions, but I thought I missed the turn." Did I oversell it? Does the K Motel even have a coffee shop? It's right on the highway, so I've driven past it many times, but don't remember seeing a sign. I give him what I hope is a winning smile and casually shift into drive.

He squirms his shoulders, then releases the door handle and gives his pants a tug. He bares his big teeth in a surprisingly nice smile, and says, "Just head back the way you come and turn west when you hit the Trans Canada. You'll come to it."

I say, "Thanks!" Even though he's close enough I might drive over his feet if he doesn't step back, I press on the gas pedal and force myself not to speed even though every nerve in my body is telling me to floor it. I don't take my hand off the steering wheel to crank the window shut until I'm past the utilities easement.

I'm over the tracks before my heartbeat returns to normal. There was no way he could harm me because I would've been blocks away before he got the door open, so what was it that made me feel threatened? Was it only my over-active imagination that set my heart thumping?

Maybe K.C. is right and I should let it go. But confronting me like that? Now I really want to know what he's protecting that he felt the need to walk half a block. I've never seen him walk farther than from his truck to his porch.

I won't mention this to K.C. because he doesn't understand my obsession with the guy, and I can't explain it. What's worse is the fact my van is burned. Next time, I'll come in my truck.

With my P.I. assignments coming in fairly regularly, I'm too busy to take another trip to Dogpatch. K.C.'s reputation as a coach and trainer means he's keeping busy, wine sales are on the uptick after winning a couple of medals at the Rocky Mountain Wine Festival, and the Bistro/farm store business is steady. Things are going well. For months we've been making our mortgage payments easily and have even paid down our line of credit. It looks like we'll weather our upcoming winter slowdown okay. Dare I believe we are finally over the hump?

Whatever was bugging K.C. seems to have passed too, and suddenly, he wants sex so often it's almost like when we first got together. As much as I worried all those weeks when he wasn't interested, this is over the top, but how do I refuse without sending him back to whatever dark place he just came out of?

He's never explained what was wrong, and I'm not about to ask. He sold the horse trailer that had been in inventory for the longest, and when he told me he now has a waiting list for horses to come in for training and has clinics booked to the end of October, he said, "That's a relief." I conclude the negativity so unlike his usual upbeat attitude was just worry about his business. There's no excuse for taking it out on me, but I won't dwell on it. Instead, I push the memory of how unpleasant it was living with him when he was like that to the farthest reaches of my mind and enjoy having the old K.C. back.

"K.C. seems happier these days, don't you think?" I ask. I'm standing beside the barbeque outside the Bistro, chatting with Stu and savouring the aroma of chickens sizzling on the rotisserie.

"Ay-yuh, think so," Stu agrees. "Sure hate to see a fella down in the dumps like that."

"Yeah, me too. It wasn't like him to be so negative about everything. Did he ever tell you what was bugging him?"

"Nope."

"Typical men. You talk about trucks, bulls and horses, never about feelings."

Stu says, "Well, if he ain't told you, you think he'd tell me?" He wipes his hand on his bib apron, smearing barbeque sauce across the "Kiss" part of "Kiss the Cook and Bring Him a Beer", picks up the squirt bottle and sends a stream of water to douse a flame on the burner.

"I suppose not."

The babble of customers with the occasional bursts of laughter, the whinnies and moos of livestock in nearby corrals is peaceful. I sip my wine and I think again of how fortunate I am to be here, the third generation of Larsens on this land. And, I guess, the last Larsen, unless I change my mind about having a baby.

I wonder if K.C. would be satisfied about the family thing if we adopted. Maybe an older kid, like Charlie and Johnny were when Stu and Red adopted them. People say older kids come with too many problems, but those boys have been nothing if not a blessing. I'm about to say something like that when the peace is shattered by a succession of motorcycles roaring by on the road.

"Jeez, what are those guys are doing out here? Wonder where they're going. Be right back." I put my wine glass down on the shelf at the side of the barbeque and go around to the street side of the Bistro, through the parking lot to the driveway and trot up to the road to look. I don't know why, really, because I expect to see them disappearing into the distance. Instead, it looks like they're turning in to the Rocking R.

Red comes out of the Bistro to join us just as I return to the barbeque. "What was all that racket?" she asks.

"A bunch of motorcycles," I reply. I pick up my wine and drain it before adding, "And their destination was the Rocking R."

"Shee-it!" Stu exclaims, "that ain't good."

No, it sure ain't.

The worst thing about the bikers is their constant coming and going. At least the South Saskatchewan Fracking trucks aren't roaring by at all hours of the day and night. It affects Red more than anyone, because the Pedersen trailer is close to the road. Stu is so deaf he could sleep through a tornado, but Red is a light sleeper.

"I guess they just showed up in combat formation the first time to make a statement," I suggest. The businesses are closed for the day and we're all on the Bistro patio for our evening conflab.

Red has never been able to sit still for long, so she's busy wiping down the tables and chairs. "Well, never thought I'd say it, but I'll be glad when the snow flies. Be glad if we ever get the money to pave our parking lot. This dust is too damn much, and it don't stay outside, neither," she says, and clicks her tongue.

"I wish you'd leave that for the morning crew, Red," I tell her. She nods, but keeps wiping.

"Wonder what's going on over at the Rocking R that causes so much traffic, day and night, anyway," I say. "You ever see what they're up to when you're over there, Stu?"

"Not since they starting building their fence," Stu replies. "Like I told you, looks like that fence is going to come right up to the barn and the sucker is damn near eight feet tall. Ask yourself, who builds a fence that tall?"

"Someone with something to hide," I conclude. "But are they leaving enough space for the bull haulers to get in and turn around?"

"Don't look like it," Stu replies.

"I bet that's the point," K.C. says.

"Already pointed that out last time I seen Trina out in the yard and talked to her, but they ain't done nothing. I've been thinking of getting outta the rough stock business, so that'll mean less bull haulers, but even so, we still got cattle to ship and there's still hay trucks and grain deliveries. I'm going to have to speak to her again," Stu says.

"Wait a minute—you're thinking you might quit supplying stock to the rodeos?" I ask. "Why?"

"Well, you said it yourself. Costs of feeding the stock and paying drivers for hauling 'em don't leave much profit. Don't know if it's worth the effort no more. Me and Red've been talking. Thinking we'll get outta it and just keep the semen business."

"I'll run some numbers, and we can talk about it," I tell him.

"Good, thanks," Stu says. "Anyhow. Time comes I have to talk to her 'bout her goddamn fence, if I know Trina, she won't see reason. She's bound to have some of them bikers around. I could use you backing me up, K.C."

"Of course," K.C. agrees.

*Of course.* "You don't really think you'll fight them? They're not schoolyard bullies, they're grown men, probably experienced streetfighters. When's the last time either of you got into a fist fight?"

"You forget back in the day, how Gorgeous loved to fight? And how his buddies—Painless and Wiggles and Melon and sometimes me and your dad—always wound up in it?"

"Yeah, you were all a lot younger then. And where's Gorgeous now?"

"Um, well…"

"Yeah. It killed him. Stu, how many concussions have you've had? Half a dozen, that you know of? The reason you quit rodeo, right? If you got punched in the head, you'd be dead, too. Or worse, you'd be a drooling idiot. Besides, you're adults, for chrissake, surely you're smarter than to get into a punch up."

Stu says, "I just meant, we might need our own show of force."

"Well, I think we just take the course of least resistance and build another road access at the south end of the barn. Then the rigs don't have to turn around. It's always been a tight fit for the B-trains anyhow, so it's long overdue."

There seems to be agreement all around. I'm not so sure Stu would back down from a fist fight, though, and K.C.? From the look of grim determination on his face, he wouldn't, either. I hope it doesn't come to that.

We've left Wacasko-Wâti in the hands of employees, and the Larsen/Garland family of two and the Pedersen family of four are at the Nekaneet Powwow. It's open to the public, so although Red and the boys are the only First Nations members of our group, there are enough white faces in the crowd that we aren't conspicuous.

This is first time we've seen Felix in his RCMP uniform. He's strolling around with Constable Butts, and we meet up with them near the hand-made dreamcatcher vendor's display. "Hey, guys!" he says.

We all mutter something in reply. Felix, the incurable tease, is now all business. The most teasing he does is to give the brim of Johnny's hat a flick.

"Hey!" Johnny exclaims, but from his big grin, he not only doesn't mind, but enjoys the attention from the cousin he's so proud of.

"Do you think there'll be problems?" I ask.

"Naw, don't think so," Felix replies. "It's a soft assignment. We're just here so there's an RCMP presence."

Gerard doesn't say anything, but since he doesn't agree, I wonder if Felix's assessment is optimistic. There's no liquor allowed on site, but that doesn't mean people can't sneak it in or arrive already drunk. Get enough drunks together and anything can happen.

"The most we might do is to stop drunks at the gate, or pour out booze we catch people with," Gerard says, as if reading my mind. "Well, folks, we gotta keep moving. Catch you later."

"Catch you later," we reply as the two officers move off toward the crowd at the bannock truck. I buy a dreamcatcher small enough to hang from my truck's rear-view mirror before we head to the viewing stands.

The boys spot kids they know from school and head off to join them, while Stu, K.C., Red and I find seats in the stands. Everyone seems cheerful and it looks like the dancing is well received. Red's sister Rose and her husband George are dancers, and we see them in the circle. The Owl Dance is a couple's dance. Several Nekaneet women go out into the crowd to find partners. We're applauding the dancers when I notice a stir at the gate. Felix and Gerard are there, blocking the entry, and their stiff body language with hands on holsters says they're in a confrontation. I dig K.C. with my elbow, point and hiss, "Look!"

Whatever the issue was, it's resolved quickly. Felix and Gerard stand aside and half a dozen men file in. Their leather vests mark them as bikers. And with them, Trina, in very short jean cut-offs, a bikini top, and cowboy boots. She has one narrow braid in her hair with a colored feather in it. Why? To make sure anyone obtuse enough not to realize from her café au lait skin, black hair and black eyes that she's native, and belongs here? Is it about her so-called blood bond with the land? If so, in my opinion she's failed and just looks like a tart.

Red draws a quick breath. I think she disapproves of Trina's outfit, but then she says, "Wonder who's looking after Newt," and starts climbing down. I follow her, with K.C. and Stu right behind me. We thread our way through the crowd until we're face to face with Trina.

"Trina! Where's the baby?" Red demands.

"Oh, hi, Mom," Trina responds, and giggles as she takes a stumbling step back, bumping into the man behind her. She reeks of liquor and might have fallen if there was no one to steady her.

"Trina, where's Newton?" Red asks again.

"I took him to the Bistro and left him with Lucy. I tol' 'em you said it was okay. You are his granny after all."

"Well, it's not okay!" My tone is harsh. One of the bikers steps up between us. Definitely an *in your face* move. I resist a strong urge to take a step back.

"None of your fucking business," he says. He grabs his crotch and adds, "Suck this."

I note his reddish beard has gray stripes running from the corners of his mouth to his chin. He's so close I can see the surgical scar from cleft palate repair under his moustache and feel his spittle on my face.

*Ewww!* I wipe my hand across my mouth before telling him, "Actually, it *is* my business. Who do you think—"

"Lindy, time to go," K.C. says. His tone is neutral, but he grips my arm upper arm so strongly it hurts. I stiffen and give my arm a jerk, but he only tightens his hold.

"Come on, Lindy," Red says. Since even she and Stu are in agreement, I stop resisting. K.C. releases my arm, but draws me into a one-arm hug that traps me at his side.

"I'll go round up the boys and meet you at the van," Red says.

Later, we're gathered around the table at Red and Stu's.

"You grabbed my arm so hard I'm going to have bruises," I complain. "What did you think I was going to do?"

"Nothing much," K.C. replies, "you'd just keep provoking him until you said something that got us into a brawl, and you recently pointed out that we should be smarter, at our age. I realize you're a few years younger than me, but I'd say you're close enough to my age to be smarter, too. Even just a bunch of yelling and Felix and Gerard would've come back. Best thing was to walk away. I know you think you're right, and I agree with you, Lindy. That guy was an asshole. I think he was hoping to start something. But we have to pick our battles."

"K.C.'s right, Lindy," Stu agrees. "We couldn't take on them guys. Six against two?"

"I know," I mutter.

K.C. continues as if I hadn't spoken: "What if you got Felix and Gerard involved? It could go real bad. We may be heading for a confrontation with those assholes, but a crowd at a pow wow isn't the time or the place."

"Goddammit, what did we do to deserve them for neighbors?" Red is rocking Newt as she gives him a bottle. The baby's eyes are half closed as he fights to stay awake. "Looking at the number of bottles and diapers she left, looks like she planned to leave him here for the night. Never even asked."

"Yeah," I say, and sigh. "I figured she'd been too quiet. Drama follows her like a bad smell."

"It sure does," Red agrees. "Them adoptive parents of hers musta really spoilt that kid."

"One good thing," Stu points out, and turns to grin at Red, "we get time with the little guy. You're happy 'bout that, right, darlin'?"

"Told her I'd take him if she needed a babysitter," Red says. "Kinda expected her to ask first. But yeah, I'm happy."

"Guess we should get the old crib down out of the loft and get it set up," Stu says, and stands. "Guess I'll go get it now."

I'm glad for Red. And I have to admit the guys are right about not letting the confrontation with the biker escalate. But Stu's comment about us heading for a confrontation with Trina and her crew niggles at the back of my mind. We came close to it today.

Trina warned us that they had a plan. But what? And when?

# Chapter 5

The day begins with frantic doorbell ringing followed by pounding on the door. I've been up for a while, but I'm still in my robe, haven't finished my first coffee, and I'm in the middle of my morning bathroom constitutional.

"Can you get that, K.C.?" I shout.

He doesn't reply, but I hear Johnny's voice. Loud. Excited. I rush to finish up and leave the bathroom without washing my hands.

K.C. is out on the porch, pulling on his boots. "What is it? What's going on?" I ask.

"One of the irrigation pipes sprung a leak and half our saskatoons are washed out," he says, and grabs a hat off the hook. "Hope the kid's exaggerating," he adds, and trots away.

I hurry to the bedroom and pull on jeans and a shirt, then fill a travel mug with coffee, and head out. I'm halfway to the field when it hits me: how does an irrigation pipe spring a leak? Even if a connection came apart, which never happens, very little water would come out unless the pump was running. And at this time of year, we don't leave it on overnight.

Red and I are standing at the edge of the saskatoon field, watching as half a dozen fieldworkers who should be harvesting rhubarb slog through the mud, salvaging saskatoon bushes and rebuilding rows. Stu and K.C. are at the irrigation hub with Cst. Gerard, mostly standing around with hands on hips, but occasionally pointing at different things and hunching down for a closer look. Now they must be satisfied, because Gerard climbs through the fence to the road where his cruiser is parked, Stu heads toward us and K.C. plows his way through the mess to the nearest couple of fieldworkers.

"This ain't good," Stu says as he comes up. "These fellas have been here for hours and now it's after lunch. They need a break and we're going to have to feed 'em. I told 'em to come to the patio on the barn side of the Bistro and you'll have burgers ready in half an hour. Okay?"

"Okay," Red says, "but keep the guys with mucky boots to that one side of the patio."

"What went wrong?" I ask. "Are the bushes we replanted going to survive, do you think?"

"Time will tell, but I think so. At least some will. Dunno how this could've happened. Good goddamn thing the pump ran outta gas or who knows how bad it might of got. Lucky the saskatoons were done for the year. As it is, next year ain't going to be good for berries. Besides that, this delays the rhubarb harvest, and it's already the end of June," Stu replies. "We should be harvesting today. Acid's going to build up worse every day we have to leave it out and it'll be sour as hell and that'll affect the wine. It'll be a while before we win any more prizes."

"I'll make some calls. See if I can get a few more people to come and pull rhubarb," I offer. "And I can pitch in. Maybe it won't be too bad."

"Give Dwight a call and see if he'll come, too," Stu says. He shakes his head and half turns away, hissing, "Goddammit!"

Why do emergencies always seem to come up when I've got so much office work? Fortunately, I manage to call in enough additional fieldworkers that Stu sends me away and I finish pushing paper by mid-afternoon. I head down to the arena, where K.C., also sent back to his regular job, is giving Ester her weekly lesson. As I come in the door and approach the wall that divides the ring from the viewing area, he notices me and gives a little nod before returning his focus to the rider. This woman is slim and fit, the horse is talented, and they're working hard to move up the ranks. In other words, she's the kind of student coaches love. I decide against asking what time he'll be done for the day and instead go back out across the parking lot to the Bistro.

As I approach the coffee bar, Marcie comes out of the kitchen to deposit fresh cinnamon buns in the pastry case. She says, "Barney thought you might not've had lunch, so he made you a Caesar salad."

"I love him," I say, and follow Marcie back into the kitchen, where the big man is scraping the grill. "Hey, Barney. Make me a nice piece of garlic toast?"

"You got it," he agrees. Caesar salad with a thick slab of Barney's salt rising bread slathered in garlic butter and grilled is the cat's meow. Even if I'd eaten lunch, I wouldn't pass it up. I grab the bowl of salad, wait impatiently for the toast to be finished, and once this meal extraordinaire is in my hands, head out of the kitchen to the staff table.

There's a tall man at the coffee bar. He's dressed in jeans, black leather jacket, and motorcycle boots. A loop of chain dangles from his hip. Biker. I glance out the window and see a motorcycle that wasn't there before I went into the kitchen. One of Trina's friends? They never come here. At least they haven't until now. My guts clench.

He turns and when he sees me, cocks his head. There's something familiar about him. Is he the jerkoff who got in my face a few days ago? No, too good looking, and no goatee. One of the others? I didn't pay enough attention to recognize any of them. He's alone. Not likely one guy would start something. Not without backup. I check the window again. Unless they're parked around the side where I can't see them, there's still just one motorcycle.

This guy's frown is more puzzled than threatening. I set my tray on the staff table, go to him and ask, "Can I help you?"

"Lindy?" he asks.

I study his face and with a shock, recognize him. "Mark?"

"My God, Lindy!" In two steps he's got me in a bear hug, swinging me around and planting a kiss on me before setting me down again. "What are you doing here?"

"I could ask you the same thing."

"Well, I was on my way across Canada—jeez, doll, if I'd known where to find you, I'd've made the trip long before now. Lost track of you and Chuck when you moved to Calgary." He takes a step toward me as if to embrace me again.

"Hey, it's been what? Ten years? More?"

"At least," he replies.

"Well, grab a coffee and sit with me while I eat my lunch so we can catch up. Can I get something for you?"

"Yeah," he says, grins and takes a breath. "I need a coffee for sure, and I'm so hungry I could eat a horse. What's good here?"

"Well, no horse on the menu, but everything is good, and our burgers are awesome. One, two, or three patties or a couple patties and a smoky. We call that bad boy our Badlands Burger.

All with or without cheese, of course. Your choice of fries or salad."

"Make it a Badlands Burger with cheese, and fries, please," he says.

"Grab one of those mugs there and help yourself to a coffee. As soon as I put your order in, I'll join you at that table," I say, and point to where I left my lunch.

I go into the kitchen to give Barney the order, then come back to the table and slide into a chair across from him. "Hope you don't mind if I start eating before you get your food," I say. "I'm starving."

"Course not. Go ahead," he says. Ordinarily it would take me under five minutes to demolish my lunch, but I feel a little self-conscious with him watching, so I slow down and poke through my salad while we chat. I tell him about the latest disaster to hit Wacasko-Wâti, and he commiserates appropriately.

He asks if I've kept in touch with any of our classmates. "No. Couple years ago, I got an invitation to the ten-year class reunion, but didn't go. René—remember her? She was organizing the thing—called to find out what my excuse was, and we caught up a little. But that's it."

"Figures," Mark says. "She was always organizing something."

"If not for her and her organizing, I doubt I would've had a social life back in the day." I don't add that it was at one of her parties that I met Chuck. And, of course, Mark. "What about you? What did you end up doing, I mean, for work?"

"Well, I work for Canada Revenue, not a bad job, great perks including a nice pension somewhere down the line. But I have a little sideline as a money manager or investment advisor, whatever term you prefer. It's my real love. I'd be happy to take a look at your portfolio for you."

"Portfolio? That's a joke!"

"Well, you'll need one sooner or later. Keep me in mind."

"I will," I promise. "Say, did your old gang stay together after grad? I mean, the group that lived in the area, at least?"

"Some of us did. At least those of us who ended up in Toronto." He rattles off half a dozen names, then asks, "You with a BBA, I sure never expected you'd end up waiting tables."

"Well, actually, my work is in the office. I mostly just show up here to eat. I'm the owner," I explain.

"Well, that's putting that business admin degree to good use. And I'm glad I caught you. But Chuck? A rancher? I never would have imagined that."

"Nope, he's city through and through. He hated it here. Called it *that rathole*."

"Rat hole? But it looks like a, er, country estate."

"Well, thanks. It was different back then, though. Nothing but a trailer, the old barn, and some corrals on a dusty gravel road. Built my house when I moved here. Couple years later, my partners and I built what started as a farmgate store for Red's pies and Stu's wine. That morphed into the Bistro. Then we added the wine tasting room, and a couple years after that, the indoor riding arena. That's the big building on the far side of the old barn."

"Impressive."

"So, what with the landscaping upgrades—lawns and shrubs and such along with the covered patios—Chuck might like it now. But we split when I moved here, and I haven't seen him since."

"Oh, um, I'm sorry?"

"Don't be. Marrying him was a mistake." I chuckle again. In all honesty, it's more of a giggle. Where is that coming from? I've never been a giggler.

"Well, anyone could've told you that," he says. "Why'd you choose him instead of me, anyhow? I'm taller, smarter, and way better looking."

"Yeah, but you were just too modest," I reply. In fact, it was a toss-up. Chuck was the smooth operator determined to get to the top of the heap, but Mark had a sort of bad boy vibe I found alluring back then. My mother's head would have exploded if I had hooked up with him. I wonder why I didn't pick him, for that reason alone. I can't tell him that, though, so I say, "Truthfully? I really don't know. I, er, um, I was stupid. That's the only reason I can come up with. What about you? Married?"

"Was," he says, and takes a sip of coffee. "She's tall and blonde, like you. That's where the resemblance ends." He gives me a look that strikes me dumb with a shocking and unexpected rush of desire. I should tell him I'm with someone. But instead, like an idiot, I stare into his eyes. They're light brown, like single malt whisky, with a few gold speckles.

Beautiful.

I don't know how long we would have locked eyes if not for Marcie coming out with his order. She scans the floor to see where to deliver the burger and does a double take when her gaze settles on Mark sitting with me.

"This must be yours," she says as she comes up beside him.

"Yes, ma'am," Mark says, and turns to her with a smile.

She sets his plate in front of him and lays the napkin-wrapped cutlery next to it.

Thank God for her timely interruption! I say, "Marcie, this is Mark, an old friend from college." I turn to Mark and tell him, "Marcie was our first employee. She helped make Red's Pies, way back before the Bistro was even a thing and we just supplied pies to a local restaurant. She's single, by the way."

"Pleased to meet you, Marcie," Mark says, and gives her a smile and a nod.

"Um, you too," she says. She blushes adorably. But Mark has turned his attention to his burger, picks it up and takes a good chomp. "*Mmm*, delicious. You weren't kidding," he reports, and takes a second bite.

Marcie hovers for a second before scurrying back into the kitchen. She must've said something the instant she got back into the kitchen, as right then, Red appears behind the pastry case and makes a show of wiping it down.

"The beef is our own. Grass fed. Not corn fed like what you get in Ontario. The smoky is made by Tony, from Tony's Deli in town," I tell him. I realize I'm jabbering, telling him all this stuff he can't possibly be interested in. I give myself a mental headshake, and ask, "So anyway, what are you doing here?"

He swallows, takes a sip of coffee, and says, "Decided I couldn't face another tax season, so I'm on sabbatical, taking a road trip. Figured it's the best way to see the country. Easy Rider, Canadian version, but without the drugs."

"Oh, yeah, um, right, I loved that movie, but you're twenty years too late."

"Better late than never, they say."

"I guess. So, which one are you, Wyatt or Billy?"

"Which one do you think is better looking?"

"Well, I always did like Peter Fonda. So, Wyatt, I guess."

"Okay, I'm Wyatt," he decides.

"Naturally. I remember you having a motorcycle, but I thought it was just, you know, cheap transportation. You're a biker now?"

"Naw, not a biker, but I always liked to ride. Up until now I've just been a weekend rider. Got some buddies I usually ride with, but couldn't convince them to come this far. They turned back at the lakehead. I didn't mind continuing on alone. You know, everywhere you go, all you gotta do is park beside other motorcycles and you've instantly got buddies. Ran into a bunch of guys I guess you'd say are the real thing at a gas station in Swift Current. We got talking. They said there's a ranch down this way hiring guys for grunt work. Room and board plus a few bucks besides. So, I thought, what the hell? I worked construction in the summer to pay for university, so I'm not completely useless. What better way to experience ranch country than working on a ranch? Figured I'd better not show up hungry, though. I was beginning to think it was a mistake to drive past that pub a ways back when I saw this place. Like the chick flicks my ex liked to watch, it's serendipity." The misaligned eye tooth does nothing to detract from the wide smile I remember so well. He dives into his coleslaw, munches, and between forkfuls says, "I'm heading for the Rocking R. You know it?"

Serendipity that he's going to hook up with that crew? What do I say to that? I manage to keep my tone neutral despite the adrenalin rush and reply, "Uh, yeah, it's just a little farther down the road. Next driveway on your right."

It takes a lot to put me off my feed, but I lay my fork down and put my napkin over my unfinished salad as I feel my face becoming flushed. He is focused on his food and doesn't notice. I was considering asking him to pitch in with the field work for a few days, but we couldn't offer him anything more permanent than that, not when we'll soon be laying people off for the season. I can't tell him not to take a job at the Rocking R because we don't like the people. Just that fast, my mood goes from *happy to see you* to *oh, shit*.

"We'll be neighbors, then," he says without looking up. "Great!"

Yeah. Great.

Red wastes no time coming to look for me as soon as Mark roars away on his motorcycle, and follows me as I'm heading out onto the patio with my mug of coffee. There are a few empty tables. I choose the one farthest from other customers, right at the edge of the patio. Red doesn't sit at the table, but hovers over me. If someone barely over five feet tall can hover. "You friendly with bikers now?"

"He's not a biker."

"Walks like a duck. Talks like a duck," she insists. "You invited him to sit with you? How come? Feel sorry for him eating alone?"

I notice Dwight with Stu and K.C. coming out of the barn, heading our way, and explain, "We were friends back in Kingston. He was Chuck's study partner. More his friend than mine." I'm uncomfortable lying to Red, because she always seems to know it. At least this is partly true. We were friends and he was Chuck's study partner. Although Chuck did most of the studying and Mark just liked hanging out at our place.

"From the look on your face, I'd say you was real good friends," Red says. "You going to tell K.C.?"

The man in question comes up beside me and asks, "Tell me what, babe?"

"Someone I knew in university showed up here," I reply. "You done for the day?"

"Ay-yuh. Friend from university? Ain't that nice," Stu says, and takes a seat across the table from me. "If you're going to get beer, K.C., bring one for this old bugger, would ya? What about you, Dwight?"

"Beer's fine with me," Dwight replies.

"You sit, K.C.," Red says. "I'll get the beer." She scurries back inside and K.C. sits beside me.

"Thanks for coming, Dwight," I say. "You're a glutton for punishment."

"What? No. It's fun driving that little gizmo. And I wanted to let you know the news about Janey."

"Oh?"

"Yeah. You wanted to know how long they figure she was killed before she was found. Apparently, she had only been dead two or three days when they found her."

"My God," Stu says.

I draw a deep breath and bite my lip to stop it quivering. Was she raped? Tortured? I can't bring myself to ask, because I really don't want to know the answer.

Red returns with a pitcher of draft and four glasses. She sets the tray down and pours, placing a full glass in front of Stu. She looks at the faces around the table and asks, "What's up?"

Stu says, "I think we could use a scotch chaser."

I get up and say, "I'll get the scotch."

Red looks puzzled, but doesn't push for more information, just fills the glasses and sits down next to Stu.

When I'm back with the scotch, I take my seat. Red looks as if she's about to cry. I guess she was given the news while I was away. To change the subject, I ask, "No more lessons today, K.C.?"

"Nope. Thought since we still got a couple hours daylight, I have time to work Rocky. He's getting too full of himself. I can't give him a day without at least some handling."

"He sure is a handful," I say.

"Ay-yuh, he's a challenge," Stu says. "K.C.'s put enough time in on him he should be further along than he is."

"True," K.C. agrees, "but what works for ninety-nine percent of colts I've started, doesn't work for him."

"What about long-lining instead of riding him, then?"

"We'll get there, babe," K.C. assures me. "Today I think I'll ride him out. I want to go see how far the runoff from the field went. Maybe it pushed enough mud down the ravine to be a good start for the little dam we talked about building. You got time to saddle Chica and come with me?"

"I do, but after the morning you've had, do you still have the energy to deal with Rocky?"

"Will, soon as I wet my whistle." He gives my forearm a rub. "You don't need to worry about Rocky, you know. I can handle anything he throws at me."

"Famous last words," I say.

"No use telling her not to worry," Stu says.

"I guess you're right," K.C. agrees, then turns to me and asks, "so, what is it about this friend that Red thinks you should tell me?"

"So, Dwight, what do you think of the draft beer?" I ask.

"Mmm, mmm. Glad you got draft beer set up. Bottle beer's nice, but nothing beats draft."

K.C. gives me a look that tells me he noticed I dodged his question, but he doesn't repeat it. Instead, he tells Dwight, "I agree. Need to get a couple more brands, though. Dunno why we went cheap and bought the single Kegerator. Could've got the four-tap model for not much more."

"We didn't buy it, you did," I remind him. "And we do have a credit limit. You just bought that AMT—"

"You said we paid down our line of credit. And everyone uses that thing. We could use another one, really. The way it is, when the field workers need it, the barn workers are using it. Look how good it worked out this morning. Dwight had it going everywhere. Nothing stops it. Could use another one for sure."

"Oh, please don't buy another one. Not right now, anyway. It is great, but we did fine before we had it."

"It's all about convenience, babe. Increased productivity. As for more beer on tap, a new dispenser would pay for itself within a month," he argues. "Siphon off some of Billie's customers."

"You don't know that would happen. I'm not saying it wouldn't, just that we need to be conservative about taking on capital expenditures at this time of year, and now this flood—"

"Besides, we're a bistro, not a dang pub," Red says. "We need a decent microwave before we spend more on draft beer."

"I'll just nip in and refill this," I say, and pick up the pitcher as I get to my feet. It's a welcome excuse to get away in case K.C. wants to know more about Mark. I'm not sure exactly what I could tell him, or what my face might give away. I don't think he needs to know how close I came to dating him instead of Chuck.

I would never cheat on K.C., but even in the midst of the flood disaster and his news he's planning to join the ranks of the enemy, I can't deny Mark's slightly crooked smile rekindled a spark that I didn't know was still there.

We ride south with the edge of the ruined saskatoon field on our right. On our left, the downhill side, workers are still pulling rhubarb and filling boxes. Everywhere there are field workers gathering the muddy blobs that are our washed-out saskatoon bushes. Harry, the straw boss, is going from collection site to collection site, loading the plants into the Green Machine and taking them back up the field to be replanted.

"Told you it was useful. Wouldn't've got nearly this much done without it," K.C. points out.

Farther on, a tractor is pushing mud around, trying to put it back where it came from. I recognize most of the workers, so they're our regular employees rather than the day workers I called in this morning. I guess it's only fair to send the day workers, rather than our permanent full-time workers, home when the bigger crew was no longer needed, but it does mean overtime rates apply. Great.

"I'm still astonished that the water could make such a mess," I say.

"Yeah, looks like flowed along between the rows until it undermined the plants, and then the whole mess just slid away," K.C. says.

"Can we do something different to make sure it can't flood again?"

"Dunno. We have to plant in mounded rows across the face of the hill or the water would just run off when we irrigate."

"Yeah. No way around that, I guess. We'll just have to make sure it can't happen again."

The horses are used to tractors and the little AMT, and do nothing more than look, until the tractor backfires, then both are startled, and give a little jump. Rocky scoots a few steps and snorts.

"Good boy," K.C. says, and scratches the big horse's withers.

When we get to the gate, I push Chica up beside it, loosen the chain, and nudge her against the gate to push it open enough for her to back through. She turns her hindquarters so she's parallel to the gate on the outside, all without me letting go of the gate. K.C. taught me how to do this because I wanted to enter trail classes or ranch riding, and they always have gates. The horse has to listen to the leg and understand when asked to move sideways and back. It's a future lesson for Rocky. I think he'll have to grow a brain first. K.C. likes him and says he's plenty smart, which is part of the problem, because being smart doesn't make a horse trainable. He has way more horse experience than I do so he's probably right. When K.C. is through the gate, I close it, and we carry on along the cow path that leads to the Badlands.

"Such a gorgeous afternoon," I say. "Wish we had time to go down into the Badlands. I think it must be a year since we went down there."

"Good idea," K.C. agrees. "I'd like to see what this guy has in him, going over rough terrain."

"Maybe next time. Let's pack a lunch and make a day of it."

"When is *next time* going to be? Any time I can take off, seems like you're out somewhere spying on people."

I can't tell from his expression if that's criticism or teasing. I do know I don't want another argument, so I don't take the bait. I nudge Chica into a jog so I'm a horse length in front of him. When we come to a fork in the path, I rein her onto the trail that leads down the ravine. Thankfully, it's too narrow to ride two abreast.

The path is a steady decline. About halfway down, it crosses the creek. It's barely a trickle at this time of year, but this morning's floodwaters made it this far. Fresh mud mixed with uprooted bushes form a natural dam where we usually ford the creek. There's a puddle on the top side.

"No use building a dam here," K.C. says. "It needs to be farther up the ravine, closer to the fields. Won't be much use for supplementing our well water this far down."

"Of course, no good could come from that washout," I agree. "Should we send someone to break it up? Might make more sense to just leave it. Like a little, um, retention pond."

"Yeah, no use spending time and energy clearing it."

Mud sucks at the horses' feet as we cross below the new retention pond to the far side of the ravine, where we continue on the path down until we reach the stand of willow, aspen and buffalo berry bushes. There's a seasonal pond here, as is usual at this time of year. It's a mere twenty feet across, and it doesn't look like any floodwater made it this far. The weeds that are supposed to be under water lie on the mud, baking in the late afternoon sun. The buzzing of insects and birdsong fills the air. Dragonflies flutter and glisten everywhere. A slight breeze stirs the pungent scent of muck and decaying slough grass. The horses go through the fetlock-deep mud without hesitation and lower their heads to drink.

"I always loved this spot," I say. "So tranquil."

"Too bad there isn't more water and less rotting vegetation," he says. "What a stench. Let's head back."

It's disappointing he wants to head back already, but I don't argue. I turn Chica to head back the way we came.

"Not that way," K.C. says. "I've seen enough. Don't need to go meandering up the ravine again. Let's go up to the trail along the road. We'll get back quicker that way." He gives Rocky a series of strong nudges to push him on through the pond. The horse responds with a sudden leap, landing with a splash in the middle before scurrying up the bank and through the willows surrounding the pond. Chica and I follow, but without the leap.

When we reach the top of the ravine, we ride side by side along the fence next to the road. In a few minutes, the Rocking R comes in view and soon its entrance is just across the road from us.

"He still feels like a coiled spring. The big jerk really needs to learn patience," K.C. says. The horse gives a tug on the reins as if irritated at being held back now that we're headed for home.

At that moment, half a dozen motorcycles come roaring out of the Rocking R driveway. Instead of turning north and away from us, they ride in circles, doing donuts, revving their engines and spinning their wheels. One drops his back wheel off the edge of the pavement and onto the gravel shoulder. When he throttles up, a spray of gravel pelts us.

"Goddammit!" K.C. swears.

Then the next biker does the same thing. Rocky rears. The instant his forefeet hit the ground, he leaps sideways, throwing

K.C. out of the saddle. He manages to cling to the horse's side and may have been able to pull himself back into the tack, but the horse bucks and leaps, then plants his feet, drops his shoulder, and runs sideways out from under him. K.C. lands in a heap and the horse gallops off, heading for home. The motorcycles roar away.

Chica dances around. "Whoa! Whoa! Whoa!" I shout. She stops and I turn to see that K.C. hasn't so much as raised his head. Fear knifes through me. I call out, "K.C.! You all right?"

He doesn't respond.

I leap to the ground and hunch over him. He doesn't open his eyes. He's breathing, though, and I call his name again. Still no reply. I slap his face and say, "K.C.! Wake up!" At last, his eyes flutter open.

"Aaaghh!" he groans, struggles to sit up, but falls back. "Jesus Christ!"

"You okay?" I demand, despite my eyes telling me he is definitely not okay.

"Goddamn it, no. Something's broken."

"Your leg?"

"Think so."

He lifts his head and shoulders, propping himself up on his elbows, while I try to slow my runaway heartbeat and carefully feel down both legs from hip to heel. "Well, no bones sticking out," I tell him. "Are you sure your leg's broken? That asshole horse buggered off, but do you think you could get on Chica if I helped you?"

"No, babe," he says. "It's more than just my leg."

I study his face. He's a few shades whiter than he should be, possibly on the verge of losing consciousness again, going into shock. What can I use to make him comfortable? Keep him warm or cushion his head? Nothing other than my shirt. I rip it off and ball it up under his head, then go to Chica, loosen the cinch, and pull the blanket out from under the saddle. It's sweaty and stinky and hairy, but it's warm and it's the best I can do. I lay it over him, covering most of his torso, and instruct him to leave his arms under it. His eyes are closed now, and his only response is a groan.

"Hold tight, sweetie. I'm going to get help." When I try to mount my horse the saddle slips, and I remember I had loosened the cinch. Cursing the delay, I push the saddle back in place and with hands made clumsy with trembling, tighten it. As soon as I'm in the saddle, I put my heels to Chica. She needs no further encouragement to gallop toward home.

I don't catch up to Rocky, but someone must have seen him come in riderless, because when I'm within sight of the buildings, I see Stu and Charlie in the AMT heading my way. They're out of it and beside me almost before I rein Chica to a halt. I was calm up until this point, but now I start sobbing.

"Okay, Lindy," Stu says. "You carry on home and me and Charlie'll go along your backtrail. We'll stay with him until—"

"No! I'm going back with you," I insist.

"Okay, but ride with me," Stu concedes. He reaches up to take hold of the waistband of my jeans and practically pulls me off the horse, then turns to Charlie and says, "Son, you take Chica home. Get Mom to call an ambulance and then she should come with blankets and a shirt for Lindy. One of you guys stick at home so's you can tell the ambulance where to go."

Charlie takes Chica's reins from me and swings up into the saddle. Almost before I realize it, he's galloping off. Stu turns to me, loops an arm around me and says, "Come on, girl. He'll be okay. Jesus!" He releases me, quickly pulls off his shirt and holds it out for me to take. "Here, get yourself in this."

"I'm okay."

"No, you ain't. Your skin's clammy and you're as pale as a plate of curdled milk. I ain't going to let you faint on me." He opens the shirt out and nearly wrenches my arm to stick one sleeve on it. "You're going to wear it, 'least 'til Red comes with one of yours and some blankets." He helps me pull the shirt on, then propels me to the passenger side of the AMT. "Hop in now, Lindy."

I settle in, grip the grab bar with one hand and hold the shirt closed with the other. Stu points the little vehicle south and hits the accelerator.

By the time we reach K.C., I've replayed the mental video of what happened a dozen times. Somewhere in the daze of things, I realize the bikers were hooting and laughing loudly enough to be heard over their engines. Scaring the horses turned out better than they expected.

Was Mark with them? I can't be sure.

# Chapter 6

D wight's replacement as NCO in Charge, Maple Creek RCMP Detachment, is Sergeant Robert Coleman. As Stu and I are ushered into his office, I'm taken aback by the sight of the diminutive man behind the desk. He doesn't stand, just looks up and says, "How can I help you?"

"Hi," I say. "I'm Lindy Larsen, and this is Stu Pedersen." I stick out my hand, but he doesn't put down the pen he's holding to reply, "I'm Sergeant Coleman. Have a seat."

So we sit as told and tell him why K.C. isn't with us.

"What could we charge them with? Scaring horses? At worst it would be a traffic violation for stunting that wouldn't stick if it was only based on your complaint. I'm afraid there's nothing criminal here."

"Well, I guess they couldn't have known K.C. would get hurt, but I bet dimes to donuts they hoped the horses would act up. And deliberately spraying us with gravel? Wasn't that an assault?" I ask.

"Or an accident," Sgt. Coleman says.

I draw a quick breath. "An accident?"

I feel Stu's hand on my arm. He says, "I doubt that, Sergeant, but I'll grant you that's what them bastards would claim. What they done to our fields, sabotaging our irrigation system, that's a different matter, though."

"True," Sgt. Coleman agrees. He listens, tapping his pen on the desk blotter, as we explain how it happened and why we think Trina is to blame. He asks, "There was a threat?"

"Yes," I reply. "Vague, but definitely threatening. She said they, her and Russ that is, have plans and before long we'll be begging them to buy us out."

"So, you think flooding your field was the plan?"

"Maybe it was only the start," I say. "Enough to make us nervous. She's surrounded by bikers, guys her husband set her up with. A notorious serial killer and gun runner's probably a big man inside. Likely has quite a following on the outside, too, and there's also the rest of his crew, the guys that never got arrested. Who knows what else they might do?"

"But how would flooding your field benefit them?"

"I think they want to put us into bankruptcy."

"Again, how would that benefit them?"

"Maybe they think if we go bankrupt, they could buy Wacasko-Wâti for a song. Russ already offered to buy us out, back when he first got sent up."

"He might think he'd be our boss then," Stu says.

"Like Trina would be a figurehead. His puppet," I explain.

"What she don't know is, the home quarter ain't officially part of the ranch. It belongs to me and Red. And Lindy, of course. So if the ranch went bust, there'd be nothing she could do to get us off that piece, and the ranch without that quarter is just land."

"Yup, at the going rate it's not even worth $500 an acre," I add. "The value is in the home quarter."

"Would she have the bucks to buy the ranch? From what you've told me, she doesn't have a job."

"That's true," I agree. "But Russ has money from his drug and gun running stashed somewhere. Both of those are cash businesses as you know."

"Hmm. So. Say you're right. How did they cause the flood?"

"Just disconnected the main pipe, and started the pump."

"It's not in a locked building? No forced entry?"

"We never thought nothing like this would happen," Stu replies.

"We're putting a tall chain link fence around it and now it'll all be locked up, that's for goddamn sure," I reply. "We'll never leave gas in the tank again, either."

"Sure," Sgt. Coleman says. "Constable Butts took a look at it when you called it in. He says there's no evidence for us to go on. The usual tool marks, yes, no tire tracks. No damage to anything other than your field."

"So there's nothing you can do?" I ask.

"Well, I'll go have a chat with Mrs. Benson, but don't get your hopes up. Sorry, can't do more than that. I've been meaning to drop by your operation anyhow. My predecessor seemed to enjoy the place."

"Still does," Stu says. "Me and him go back about forty years. He spends so much time there now it's a wonder his wife ain't divorced him."

"Expect to stay for a coffee," I tell him.

"I'll do that," he says.

Back in the truck, I ruminate over our conversation with Sgt. Coleman. "There's a guy with no social skills," I say. "Surprising for one in his position."

"You're just used to Dwight," Stu says. "He'll warm up once we get to know him better."

"I hope we never get to know the little pip squeak better. You know, small man syndrome. You being a strapping six-footer intimidated him. That's why he didn't bother to get up. I bet he's incompetent."

"You're just pissed because he didn't agree with you."

I give Stu a frown, but otherwise ignore his criticism, and continue, "You know the Peter Principle? Promoted to his level of incompetence. You know who he reminded me of? Deputy Rosco P. Coltrane on Dukes of Hazzard. I half expected him to giggle."

"Well, whatever you think, it don't do no good to poke him."

"You're right," I say, and sigh. I mentally review our meeting with Sgt. Coleman. Stu's comment about the home quarter being on a separate title and without it, the ranch is just land went right by me when he said it, but now it pops into my mind.

"Stu," I say, "are you sure Trina, er, Russ maybe, neither of them knows the home quarter is separate from the rest of the ranch?"

"Dunno for sure," he replies. "Why?"

"I just thought of something. I figured if they wanted to get their hands on the ranch, they'd steal our cattle. But that's work for cowhands, and cowhands they ain't. It would be quicker and easier to knock the Bistro, and the winery, out of commission. Right?"

"Ay-yuh, like Jake nearly done."

"Don't remind me," I say, and wince at the reminder I was stupid enough to have what I thought was a serious relationship with a con man. "But he had big money bosses behind him. He was just their flunky. Like Trina and her bikers are Russ' flunkies. Destroying our source of produce for both the wine and Red's Pies may only be the start. Then maybe they realized just doing that would take too long. They may be planning something with more immediate results."

"You're worrying too much. What're they going to do? Burn down the Bistro?"

"Maybe."

"They wouldn't do that," Stu says. "And if they did, our insurance would replace it. Right?"

"Sure, but if it was arson and they could somehow pin it on us, bye-bye insurance money. Even with the insurance money, in the time it took to rebuild, we might be bankrupt. And I bet Russ has enough bucks stashed away to replace it."

"But we ain't going to go bust just losing the Bistro. We ran without it for years. We'll be okay as long as we have cattle."

"And if our herd got infected with mad cow disease again, or there's brucellosis—"

"My God, girl! You gotta be the world's biggest worry wart. Our cows never got the mad cow disease."

"They did, though. Not until after Jake's big shot money friends seized them, but they got it. Remember? At the time, we thought it was justice."

"Okay, sure, then, if you're determined to drive yourself crazy with worry." He downshifts as we approach our driveway, then turns to look at me and adds, "But there ain't been a case of brucellosis in Saskatchewan in years. 'Member? The government declared Saskatchewan brucellosis-free."

"Yeah. But what about that new bison ranch just west of the Rocking R? They could bring it in."

"You know them buffaloes had to be vet checked before they could be moved anywhere. But since you're determined to worry, you know how close we are to AFB Cold Lake? They think the UFOs are attracted to air force bases, and that's why everyone's been seeing them there. A UFO wouldn't take more'n the blink of an eye to fly right here and beam all our cattle up. Maybe they need the meat to feed their crew. And I suppose there's always a chance our cows could get wiped out if one of 'em was to crash."

Stu, ever the optimist and me, ever the worrier. No use talking about it. But I'm going to check our insurance papers, and if need be, increase our business interruption coverage. I think of how we deliberately chose all that cedar—shake roof, siding, pergola, even interior finishes—because it looks rustic and suits ranch buildings, never taking into consideration how well it burns. As happy as I am to see our line of credit trending downward and even with expenses for a new pump for the irrigation system in the offing, I think it's time the Bistro had a sprinkler system.

Without K.C., Wacasko-Wâti seems empty. Without K.C., I'm empty. It's not like he hasn't been away before, even for weeks at a time like when he worked at Douglas Lake Ranch our first summer together. Since then, he goes away when he's got a clinic or is judging a show, but somehow, this is different.

The last time I visited him at the hospital in Saskatoon, the doctor said he would be there a few more weeks, and then he'd be transferred to a rehab facility in Regina. It takes over three hours to drive to either city, so it'll still take a day to visit him. Due to the severity of his injuries, it's expected to take four to six months for him to heal, although he can come home for most of that. The bad news is it could be a lot longer than that before he puts a leg over a horse again, and he'll set off metal detectors and walk with a limp for the rest of his life.

I get off the elevator and head for Room 1022. Last time I visited, I expected him to be grouchy like he was a few weeks ago, but he was so cheerful and pleasant I could barely believe it. Now I hear laughing and there's feminine giggling. He's in a semi-private room, so it could be the guy in the next bed who's flirting with a nurse, but my money is on K.C.

I imagine the nurses all love him. Who wouldn't love a guy who's tall (although I guess they can't tell since he's flat on his back with one leg wrenched up in the air), good looking, has a brilliant smile (if you can see it through that contraption that's immobilizing his head), is quick with a compliment, the master of the risqué remark, and is completely at your mercy? Handcuffed to the bedpost times ten, without the sex, although we've all heard jokes about nurses and sponge baths. It's me who's down in the dumps. Which is not to say I want him to be miserable. But does he have to be so thrilled?

He's not thrilled. That's a mean thought. It's just that I might feel better if he was as depressed as I am at his, I mean *our*, prospects going forward. I can't help but wonder what this does to his business and what the impact on Wacasko-Wâti will be. The ruined fields are problem enough. We really didn't need him out of commission and not generating income. How will he pay his child support and alimony? Will I have to cover it?

In fairness, I haven't told K.C. the pump had burnt out when it pumped the well dry or that we're worried the well might not recover. I haven't shared my fears there's worse to come from Trina, either, or that our line of credit will nearly be maxed out by the new security cameras and sprinkler system protecting the Bistro. I was the one yammering about no new capital expenses as we're heading into our slow season. There's nothing he can do about any of it. He needs to concentrate on getting well.

Before this happened, K.C. had clinics booked in half a dozen locations, the barn full of horses for training, and a full slate of lessons most days of the week. Now the clinics are canceled, the horses in for training have been sent home, and all his students have been told he won't be able to teach for an undetermined length of time. A few have already moved their horses out, and

I expect the rest will follow. K.C. knows all this, yet he doesn't seem concerned. I'm the bean counter, so maybe I worry about the bottom line more than most, but he's just come out of a long depression I thought was caused by worry over his business. Now this injury tanks his business, so why is he over the top cheerful?

Still, my spirits are buoyed by the sounds of laughter. I enter the room and see K.C. grinning, the guy in the next bed with a thermometer sticking out of his mouth, and a nurse standing over him. He must have been fooling with the thermometer, because the nurse says, "If you keep taking that out, I'll put it somewhere that's not as easy for you to reach."

"Maybe that's what he's hoping for," K.C. says. The two men chuckle. The nurse might be trying to look stern, but her little smile gives her away. Then K.C. spots me in the doorway. "Oh, hi, babe!"

"Hi, sweetie," I reply, go to his bedside, take his hand, and lean in for a kiss. "How're you doing today?"

"I'm fine, just fine," he assures me. "The doc says they're sending me to Regina tomorrow."

"That's good news," I say. "Any updates on how long you'll have to be there?"

"Nope. I guess they'll tell me more once the docs there have a chance to check everything out. But at least I'll be able to get out of bed once they take me down off the rack." With a lift of his hand, he indicates the pulley system his leg is suspended from.

"That'll be a good thing. You must be bored stiff."

"Well, now that you're here, something's stiff, anyhow," he murmurs, and winks. Then chuckles and asks, "How're things at Wacasko-Wâti?"

"Okay. Everyone misses you, of course. And we've been talking about what to do with Rocky."

"Don't do anything with Rocky. We'll figure out something. No hurry."

"But he's dangerous."

"Not really. No one needs to handle him. He can just have a few months off. Consider it more growing-a-brain time. Leave him out with the herd."

"He's already five. When's he going to grow a brain? And you said yourself, dropping his shoulder to make sure you went off was dirty."

"Yeah. But it wasn't his fault I got hurt. Wouldn't have, if I'd missed that damn rock I landed on. Pull the curtain, would you?"

I put the box containing the two-bite meat pies we affectionately call rat turds and a couple of cinnamon buns on his bedside table next to a vase of flowers. "Here's what you asked for from the Bistro," I say, and tug the curtain around so we have a private area only slightly bigger than the bed. "Who's the flowers from?"

He hesitates for a second before replying, "My ex."

"She's just getting around to sending them now?"

"No, she was here. Brought the kids yesterday."

"Oh. That was nice."

"Sure." He pats the bed beside him and says, "Now hop up here, babe. I got an itch I need scratched."

I climb up as instructed and we snuggle as much as possible, given the contraptions he's confined in. He takes my hand and pulls it under the covers.

"*Mmmmm.* Now *that's* better," he says.

"You know I can still hear you," the man in the next bed calls out.

On my return from the hospital, I nip into the Bistro for a cup of coffee and find the kitchen abuzz. Reason: the new microwave.

"Ain't it a beauty?" Barney asks. "Way faster than the old one, and it cooks more evenly, too." He's using a dish towel to wipe smudges no one else can see.

"When did it come?" I ask.

"Johnson's brought it with their delivery," Barney says. "Paperwork's in the clip with the rest of your stuff."

I fetch my clipboard off the hook by the telephone. There it is. Damn lousy time to come off backorder now. Isn't that always the way? Looking at it now, already set up and working, I guess it's too late to return it.

"Stu's putting up a shelf in the tack room so the old microwave can go there," Barney says, breaking into my thoughts. "The boys are stoked because now they can make popcorn out there. It'll mean the hands don't need to come in here to warm up their lunches, too, so I'm pretty stoked about that."

"Good," I mutter, and muster a smile, thinking *it's only a thousand dollars... It's only a thousand dollars.*

We're around the table at Red's. The dinner things are cleared and the dishwasher's loaded. Now we're enjoying pie and coffee before night check. "I didn't see Rocky out with the herd when I drove in," I say. "Did you move him on?"

"Naw, he's out there, you must of just missed him," Stu replies. "And moved on? To where? We're still tryin' to figure out what to do with him."

"I can work him," Charlie says.

"You ain't' gettin on that horse," Red declares.

"Well, we can't sell him. He's too unpredictable," I say. "I hate to say it, but maybe it was a mistake taking him off the meat truck."

"I know you're mad at the horse, Lindy," Stu says, "but it ain't his fault, and no horse deserves that."

"That's what K.C. said. Like it was purely accidental, and he wouldn't've gotten hurt if he hadn't landed on a rock pile."

"I'd say ship them dang motorcycle guys," Red says. "That's what set him off. And from what you said 'bout them hootin' and hollerin', they were damn happy about it. And the goddamn racket, blaring their music till all hours. Just as well we got Newt here so much. What with all the goings on there, would they even mind him?"

"He's better off here," I agree.

"Why're them assholes still racing around here on motorcycles, anyway?" Stu wants to know. "I thought they gave it up and took to using their trucks instead."

"Maybe it's the last hurrah before the snow flies," Charlie says. "There's more of 'em than ever these last few weeks. Some kind of biker party every weekend. Seems like them fracking crews fit right in."

"Why do you say that, Charlie?" I ask.

"Seen their trucks there a lot. You might not of seen 'em 'cause you ain't working over there, but ain't you seen 'em on the road?"

"I guess I have. Didn't realize that's where they were going, though. That's all we need, roughnecks swelling their ranks. But you're right, Red. I'd like to get rid of the whole mob along with the horse. Dunno how to do that, either."

"Far as Rocky goes, he ain't doing nothing to bother us," Stu says. "Them bikers is another matter, but what can we do 'bout them other than wait and see what they do next?"

"Hope for the best, plan for the worst?" I ask.

"Yup. Which is what you done, getting the building sprinklered and that security camera put up," Red says.

"One security camera on the barn that looks out over the yard isn't going to do anything other than show us who might've been around, after the fact. It's that 'Smile! You're On Camera' sign in the window that's the real deterrent," I say, and add, "hopefully."

Just then, we hear a vehicle and look up to see a familiar pickup drive past the window to pull up beside the deck. In a moment, there's a tap on the door and Felix, in uniform, steps in. "Hey, everyone," he says. We all chime our hellos. Newt crawls toward him, sits and reaches up, saying, "Zoah! Zoah!"

"Hey, big guy," Felix says, and picks him up. "You have a good day?"

Newt gurgles something in reply as a long string of drool runs down his chin. I get up and reach for the baby. "You better hand him over before he slobbers all over your uniform," I say. Felix kisses the baby's head and passes him to me.

"How come he's here again?" Felix asks. "What's Trina's excuse this time?"

"Oh, the usual. She had things to do. Lots of stops to make. Too much trouble having to get him in and out of the truck a bunch of times. Won't be home until late. So I don't expect she'll come to get him until sometime tomorrow."

"She takes advantage," Felix says.

"I don't mind," Red assures him, and gets to her feet. "Cuttin' back my hours at the Bistro so I have time. Never thought I'd have a baby to look after, so it's a real gift. Have a seat. You eaten yet?"

"Now that you mention it, no I ain't," he says, and chuckles. "Any grub left, Auntie? Or have them two walking stomachs you call your sons ate it all?"

"You're still a walking stomach yourself," Red says. "You know I always cook lots. Sit, and I'll fix you a plate."

Felix slides into the spot just vacated by Red. "Any more problems with your neighbors?" he asks.

"No. Unless they done something we ain't noticed yet," Stu replies.

"Don't even want to ponder what they might come up with next," Red says. "Damn dogs never made a sound while them assholes was doing their evil business with the pump." She scrapes the last of the gravy out of the roaster over the mounds of potatoes and meat on a plate and sets it in front of Felix. "There's more meat and spuds, but that's it for the gravy," she tells him.

"This is great, Auntie. Thanks," Felix says, and digs in.

"The pump is quite a ways from the yard, here," I point out. "Henry barked. But he's half blind and getting so senile he barks at the boots on the porch, so we just told him to shut up and didn't think any more about it. Maybe it's time to quit shutting the dogs in the porch overnight," I suggest.

"Maybe," Stu agrees, "but the boys seen cougar sign last week, and we don't want them tangling with that cat and winding up gutted. Plus you know they ain't going to guard against UFOs."

"UFOs? What about UFOs, Dad?" Johnny asks.

Stu shrugs, winks at me, and says, "Nothing, son. Forget it."

Felix looks as though he might be wondering about the UFOs, too. He gives his head a slight shake and focuses on his dinner again. Then between mouthfuls, he looks at me and says, "Heard you were out to visit K.C. today, Lindy."

"Yeah. Got home just in time for dinner," I reply.

"How's he doing?"

"Fine. He's a comedian, entertaining everyone. Has the nurses falling over themselves to do his every bidding."

He barks a laugh and says, "Well, you gotta get your jollies when you can. So. You talk to him about what he wants to do with Rocky?"

"Yeah. He says to leave him be, for the time being, anyhow, and I shouldn't blame the horse. But I can't help it. I do blame him."

"Well, I been thinking, how be if I try my hand with him?"

"No, goddammit! My guys ain't getting on that horse, and you ain't neither, Felix," Red says.

"I may dress like a cop these days, but underneath, I'm still a bronc rider, Auntie. And don't worry. I don't mean trying to make a dressage horse for a lady to ride like what K.C. had in mind. I'm thinking, why don't we take him over to the Rocking R, put him in the bucking chute, and see if he's got the right stuff to make a bronc? Maybe he'd be a good fit for your rough stock herd, Uncle Stu."

"Hmm. Interesting idea," Stu says, "but I'm looking to wrap that business up, not take on more stock."

"You kidding? You'll quit the rough stock?"

"Ay-yuh. I've been sending out feelers to see if anyone's interested, but so far, no takers."

"Well, that's the first I heard of it," Felix says. He frowns in concentration as he focuses on mopping his plate with a slice of bread. When he's done with that, he leans back in his chair and says, "We should talk."

# Chapter 7

$M$ark comes in for a cinnamon bun and coffee a few mornings a week. He may have come across as a biker when he showed up here, but now he's starting to look and act like a cowboy. He hasn't been in for a few days, so we expect him this morning. The senior's coffee and chinwag regulars left half an hour ago. This time of day is usually quiet, so it's staff coffee break time.

"Doesn't look like Mark's coming today, either," Marcie says. "Wonder what cowboy gear he's going to show up in next. I bet he trades his motorcycle boots for cowboy boots."

"I doubt it," Barney says. "Working over there for Trina gets him bed and board, but I doubt she pays much, and boots're expensive."

"If I know Mark, he would've saved enough to finance two years off before he went on a one-year sabbatical," I say.

"Why would he buy boots now, when he ain't staying long?" Red says. "Now that I think about it, he's going to have a lot of stuff to pack up on that motorcycle when he leaves."

"Maybe he's changed his mind about moving on," Marcie suggests.

"Like maybe he's found a reason to stay?" I chuckle and give her a look. "Must be some reason he comes in here so often. I don't know... *Marcie McKenzie* has a nice ring to it, don't you think?"

Marcie blushes. Red gives me a strange look, and says, "Pretty sure he's got his reasons."

Coffee break is over and we're getting ready to head back to work when a truck pulls up to the edge of the patio. Mark climbs out from behind the wheel and Red exclaims, "Well, I'll be go to hell."

When he comes inside, I say, "Hey, Mark. Nice truck. Yours?"

"It sure is," he replies.

We all go outside and stand around *ooohh-ing* and *ahhhh-ing* over his truck. Barney asks about gas mileage, engines, torque and whether Chevy is better than Ford or Dodge. When the others go back to work, Mark and I move to a table out on the sunny side of the patio.

"I must say I'm surprised you'd trade your motorcycle for a truck," I tell him.

"Well, I won't need the motorcycle if I have a truck," he explains as he peels a section off his cinnamon bun and butters it. "I'd have to have transportation when the bike was put away for the winter. This way, it's gone, and I don't have to worry about it. Also made a decent trade-in. Made good sense financially."

"But I thought you loved your bike."

"I did. But lately I just haven't been feeling it, you know? Maybe I'll get another one in the spring."

"So, you're staying until spring? I didn't realize Trina's projects were... I mean, she's keeping you on all winter?"

"Don't know yet."

I don't know what to say. If he gets laid off, he'll have to go somewhere. We're one of the biggest employers around and we can't take him on at this time of year. Realistically, he should get on with his Easy Rider tour, and instead he sells his motorcycle?

I mull this over while I watch him polish off his pastry. "Can I get you more coffee?" I ask.

"Yes, please," he responds.

I take his mug and mine, refill both, and when I return, say, "I thought you said that bike was special. It won't be that easy to replace, will it?"

"Well, no. A vintage 1947 Indian Chief complete with war bonnet headlight doesn't come along every day. But it's just a thing. And maybe my motorcycle riding days are over, anyhow. Could be I was having a mid-life crisis like my ex claimed."

"A little early for a mid-life crisis, isn't it?" I ask.

"Thank you," he says.

I check my watch. "Where does the time go? I have a lot of office work, so I'd better get back to it. Have to go, Mark," I say, and get to my feet.

"Okay," he says, then narrows his eyes and asks, "say, where is it you go after the Bistro closes, Lindy?"

What? He can't see our place from the Rocking R. How does he know I go somewhere after we close? A chill spreads through me. Then, I remember he's a friend and take a breath. "What are you talking about?"

"I mean, a couple of the guys said they've seen you leaving, like you're heading into town, maybe nine, ten o'clock."

"No one can see our place from Trina's," I say.

"No, but some of the guys hang out at Billie's and they've seen you drive by. They figure you have a boyfriend in town, since K.C.'s been laid up."

"That's crazy."

"Okay, so no boyfriends. At least not to speak of," he says, with a wink and a chuckle.

"If you must know, I take the deposit to the bank."

"At night? Alone? Lindy, is that a good idea?"

"I'm careful. I don't go at the same time every night. I don't even go every night."

"So, you keep the cash in the store?"

I draw a deep breath. How did I get sucked into telling him something that's none of his business? When I don't answer, he asks, "Something wrong?"

"Why are you asking, Mark?"

"Oh. I see. You think I'm going to—"

"What else *can* I think? Maybe you'd like to know which stagecoach brings the gold for the payroll?"

"You think... Jesus, Lindy! How can you even think that?"

"People change. I don't know who you are now. And you're over in the enemy camp, after all."

"The enemy camp? They're enemies? I've figured out there's bad blood between you, but it's not like they talk about you other than the odd mention. Think of all the time I spend here—"

"I've got work to do." I turn on my heel in such a hurry that I slop my coffee, and head across the patio, into the parking lot, and up to my house. All the time he spends here? A few lunches or coffee breaks or the occasional dinner can't make up for the hours he spends with Trina's crew. I could kick myself for telling him about the bank deposits. "Stupid, stupid, stupid!" I mutter.

Before K.C lived here, I worried about going to the night depository alone, so I got a Glock to keep in the glove box. It's registered, and I spent time at the gun club learning how to shoot and practicing on their range. Turns out I'm a lousy shot, so I crossed my fingers I'd never have to use it, or if I did, that the noise would be enough to scare them off. This is Canada. Small town Canada at that. There hasn't been a robbery in Maple Creek in decades. Maybe never, even. When Dwight told us about the rash of thefts from parked vehicles, I decided it was ridiculous to keep it in the truck. It seemed more likely the gun would be stolen before I ever needed it, so I took it out.

It's time to put it back.

I'm just getting off the phone when the doorbell rings. It's a rare thing and startles me. I hope it doesn't take long to get rid of whoever it is, because I'm anxious to go find Red or Stu and give them the good news. Armed with reasons for not wanting whatever they're selling, I open the door partway. But it's not someone peddling magazine subscriptions or religion, it's Mark, cowboy hat in hand.

"Hi, Lindy," he says. "Red said you were up here, and it was okay for me to come up."

"What's up?"

"Well, I, er... I mean, it seemed like last time I was here, I made you mad. I don't want to leave it like that, Lindy. I've called and left a couple of messages, but you haven't called me back."

I sigh and pull the door open. "Come in, Mark," I say. "I don't have cinnamon buns, and my coffee's an hour old, so maybe we should go down to the Bistro."

He steps inside, smiles and says, "Here's fine."

I close the door behind him. He stands, shifting his weight from foot to foot and puts his hat on, only to take it off again as he looks around and says, "Nice house."

"Thanks. Hang your hat on the hook, there, if you want. Then go ahead and take a seat," I tell him, and gesture to the stools at the island. "I don't have cream, but I've got Coffee Mate, or there's milk."

"Coffee Mate's good," he says.

By the time I've got two mugs of coffee poured, he's settled at the end of the island. "Here you go," I say, and set his mug and a spoon in front of him. "Sugar and Coffee Mate's on the Lazy Susan." I take the stool kitty-corner from him.

"So Lindy," he says, spinning the Lazy Susan until the sugar bowl's in reach, "am I right? You're mad at me?"

"I was."

"But you know I'd never—"

"Something you might not remember about me, Mark," I interject, "is my suspicious nature. A few times now, my suspicions have proven right, so I pay attention to them. I don't know you, and I'm not the same person you knew back in university, either."

"But Lindy—"

"I didn't call you back because you're at Trina's. Should I call you there? Do you really want them thinking we're friends?"

"Well, um, doesn't matter to me. They make comments about me coming over here, but they figure I'm after a piece of tail. I tell them it's nicer and closer than Billie's and the food's good, but they don't believe that's the reason. I don't think you want them hanging around here anyway, so I don't push it and mostly just ignore them. Trina would've fired me before now if it wasn't for the bikers not being there full time and she likes having a man around. For security, you know."

"So now you're working security. Don't tell me she's never hit on you."

"Well..."

"Anyhow, I knew the bikers weren't there full time, but I guess I never thought about it. They must have jobs. Where do they work?"

"Dunno about all of them, but one guy owns a muffler shop, and they talk about an auto wrecking business. It's called B & E Auto Wrecking, sort of thumbing their noses at the cops.

They're more like mechanics than carpenters. My experience working construction in university means I know more than they do about building. Whether they like it or not, that makes me their boss."

"What are you building?"

"Couple sheds. A canopy over the new basement entrance. But the big thing we're working on now is a roof for the patio, like a big gazebo. You know. For all the guys to hang around. Not so much now, but Trina's got big plans for next summer. It's already pretty well a non-stop party."

"Yeah, we can hear the music from here." I'd like to know where the money comes from. I consider asking him, but decide against it, not wanting to sound too interested. I let it pass and to change the subject, ask, "When the construction projects are finished, and say she gets one of the bikers to stay full time, what will you do? Give up your Easy Rider adventure and drive your truck back to Toronto?"

"Might sell it and fly back if I can't find other work around here. Haven't decided yet," he replies, adds sugar and Coffee Mate to his coffee and stirs, the spoon clinking musically while he avoids eye contact.

I give him a minute, then say, "Anyhow, besides that, I'm mad at myself. I worked at a bank. I know better than to blab about cash handling procedures. At times I've worried that the young hooligans that hang around Fast Eddy's pool hall down the alley from the bank might get wind of me making bank deposits after hours. They could easily mob me. I'm thinking of one in particular. His father is in jail because of me."

"Really? How'd you manage that?"

"Long story and not something I like to talk about. But believe me, he'd mug me even if there was no money. Trina's crew wouldn't think it was worth the risk for credit card slips that wouldn't do them any good, checks they couldn't cash, and a few bucks, but they might blab, and those little shits at the pool hall could find out." I'm lying. It's more than a few bucks or I wouldn't make the trip to town. I may not be mad at Mark anymore, but I don't trust him, either. All Trina's thugs have to do to find out where I'm going, if they're really all that interested, is follow me. Now Mark can tell them the cash deposits are small.

"Sounds like you've had some misadventures," Mark says.

"You don't know the half of it," I agree.

"But what I was worried about is you going somewhere alone, what with K.C. away."

"I don't have a boyfriend, Mark."

"Not that. What I was going to say is, with K.C. away, I could take his place. I mean, if you have to go somewhere at night, I could ride shotgun. When I brought it up last time, I didn't know where you were going or why. And now, with you making the bank deposits, even more reason. And with that abduction, so close—"

"What abduction?"

"You haven't heard? It was on the news earlier."

"I, er, haven't had the radio on yet this morning. An abduction?"

"A woman, in her early twenties, I think. According to her roommate, she went out for cigarettes and hasn't been seen since."

The stupidest, most inappropriate thought pops into my head. *Smoking will kill you.* Fortunately, it doesn't come out my mouth, maybe because my stomach is clenching, and I feel my heart beginning to thump. I ask, "Where?"

"Right here in town."

Disjointed thoughts tumble through my brain. This is close to home. It's my territory. Is a gun in the glove box of any use? I've seen Big Belly Boy cruising through town. Is this latest woman still alive, or has she already been murdered? It's overwhelming. I plant my elbows on the counter and cover my face with my hands.

Mark interrupts my jumbled thoughts. "So when I came here the other day, I wanted to let you know that if you have to go anywhere at night, I'll go with you. It's even more important now. At least until K.C. is back."

I give my face a rub, then drop my hands and straighten up. "Thanks, Mark. Good of you to offer, but K.C. is coming home."

# Chapter 8

I thought K.C. being home meant things would return to normal. Boy, was I wrong. Gone is the cheerful, teasing guy he was when I visited him at the hospital or the rehab center. Back again is the guy who can't find anything positive to say about anything and might not even get out of bed if he didn't have to go to the bathroom. Thankfully, he's never asked me to bring him the bedpan. I think he might if he didn't know he'd have to be a quadruple amputee before I'd agree.

I thought that before they released him, he'd be well on the road to recovery. He's a young, healthy, strong man in the prime of life after all. The physical therapist thought he wouldn't need a wheelchair at home, but he hasn't given it up. The house isn't big, but I always thought it was roomy. Now it feels crowded. I wish he'd learn how to navigate the hallway, so he'd quit gouging the walls. I have to bite my tongue not to yell at him when he crashes into the fridge because he can't negotiate the turn into the kitchen.

He has periods of blurry vision, suffers debilitating headaches thanks to his severe concussion, and still has intense body pain besides. It's a good thing the docs gave him an open prescription for pain killers, because he's going through them the way judges of the chili competition at the Fall Fair eat antacid tablets. I'm at the pharmacy every time I go to town. And as far as riding shotgun with me when I take the deposit to the bank, he won't leave the wheelchair long enough to go down the steps, let alone to get into the truck. He'd be useless if I got into trouble anyway. The Glock is in the back waistband of my jeans on those trips now.

Today, I fool around doing busy work at the Bistro, wiping this and that and circulating with the coffee pot to top up mugs while watching for the physical therapist to come out of the house. When I see her putting her things in the trunk of her car, I hurry out to catch her.

"How is he today, Georgia?" I ask.

"About the same, I'd say," she responds.

"Yeah, I don't see much improvement, either. Is there something else wrong? I mean, I know sometimes the screws can cause problems and he's got a whack of them. I was wondering if that could be what's causing him so much pain."

"I don't know. He has an appointment with the surgeon next week. You going with him?"

"Of course."

"You should ask him. He probably needs current radiographs, so then he'll know if it's the screws." If her smile is intended to be encouraging, it's not working.

"But it's been so long and he's still using that wheelchair."

"I noticed that. And he seems to be taking an awful lot of oxycodone. He told me how often he takes a pill, but in my experience, people tend to under-report. I thought he'd be weaning off that by now."

"Should I quit getting it for him?"

"No, he's the best judge of when he needs it. But he's so negative. You know about the power of positive thinking?"

"He's positive he can't do anything," I say. "I'd be depressed, too, if I was in the horse training business and was sidelined for this long. And he's used to being so active. It's tough being tethered to the house."

"Oh, so he's not off his meds or anything? All I saw on his table was the oxy."

"Er, his meds?"

"According to his chart, Lithium. Fluoxetine. Olanzapine."

I don't know about the last two, but I recognize lithium. "Lithium? Isn't that for, um, depression?"

"That's right."

"He's not depressed, really, just feeling low. Worrying about his business. He'll get over it. He always does."

"Bipolar personality disorder is more than just low feelings, Lindy, and it doesn't get better by itself. And he always gets over it? So, this isn't the first time, then. Can't all be blamed on not being able to train horses. That's why his therapist in Katawasis Lake prescribed the meds in the first place."

I feel as if the ground is opening up beneath my feet. My legs are wobbly. I collapse back against Georgia's car.

***

Another term I picked up from my lawyer friend is *malingering*. Beer Belly Boy, sure, but K.C.? I can't believe it, but I think that's what he's doing. I keep telling myself he could never be that guy. Not him, so active and athletic and with so many plans. Still, the thought niggles at me. I decide I'm not going to be his enabler.

I refuse to have a ramp built so he can wheel himself outside, and I've told him that if he wants to eat, he's going to have to get himself onto a stool at the island. No more tray on his wheelchair. He agreed to push his chair up to the dining room table, and I agreed that was a reasonable short-term compromise. Am I being unrealistic? Maybe even mean? I prefer to call it KITA—Kick In The Ass—motivation. After a lot of grumbling because he can't see the TV, he's at the table now.

Lunch is roast beef sandwiches just the way he likes them, a nice thick filling of shaved beef with horseradish and mustard in the mayonnaise (thank you, Barney), a pickle, a cookie, and coffee. I'm sitting opposite him, enduring his complaints while we eat together. When he's quit bellyaching about how this and that hurts and has a mouthful so he can't talk back, I say, "So, sweetie, what's this I hear about you having a therapist?"

He's so surprised he stops chewing for a second, then slowly chews again before swallowing. He says, "Georgia had no business telling you."

"I'm glad she did, because we have to talk about it. Why have you never told me about this bipolar thing?"

"Because it's ancient history. I'm cured."

"From what Georgia told me, it's a lifelong condition. When you're feeling good, you might think you're cured, but you're not. I need to know what I can do to help you—"

"Help me? How?"

"Well, I'd like to meet with your doctor and find out what to expect and what I can do to help. Maybe just having someone to talk to about how you're feeling. And I could monitor your meds, make sure you don't forget. Accidentally miss a dose—"

"You can stop right there! You're starting to sound like my ex. I'm not going back on the meds. I took them for years, even after I moved to Katawasis Lake, because she insisted. I felt shitty all the time and it didn't satisfy her anyhow, as you know, since we were done long before you showed up. You don't keep taking antibiotics once your infection's gone, do you? I'm just fine. Now, why don't you take your sandwich, go back to your lair, and leave me in peace."

I know I shouldn't react. I should say positive things in a neutral tone. I reply, "You can really be an asshole, you know?"

Red is one of my two best friends. I may be the only person alive she's told the reason for her nickname when she hasn't got a single red hair or freckle. I've told her my secrets as well. She's great to have as a confidant. We're at the Rocking R, sitting on the fence, waiting for Felix and his pals to get Rocky settled in the chute on the far side of the corral. Felix is going to ride, a fact that has stoked so much fear in Red that I didn't expect she would want to watch, but here she is.

It's not just Rocky they're going to ride today, but a few of the other broncs and a couple of bulls, too, because Felix is the new proprietor of the rough stock business and wants to get firsthand experience with his animals. It's a mini-rodeo, free attendance, towns people and folks from the Rez make up the fair-sized crowd. Felix invited some of his rodeo friends to participate, so the near pasture is crowded with truck and trailer rigs in addition to the spectators' vehicles.

The cowboys are all over by the chute. Three pick-up riders are on horses in the corral, and besides Felix getting ready to climb down onto the horse, Stu and a couple other cowboys are on the rails to get his rigging secured and the flank strap set. Mark is manning the catch pen gate. There are so many people lined up along the fence we were lucky to get a good spot.

No one is near enough to overhear us so I take the opportunity to say, "Red, can I talk to you about K.C.?"

"What about him?" she asks.

"His, er, mental illness."

"Mental illness?"

"You must've noticed how withdrawn, or not just withdrawn, but how grouchy and cranky he can be? You'd think he'd be here today, but he bitched about the stairs and says it's too hard to get into the truck. I think it's an excuse. He just didn't want to make the effort. Now that he's finally given up the wheelchair in favor of crutches, I thought for sure he'd come."

"Yeah. Despite what Rocky done to him, he likes the horse, and I'd of thought he'd want to see how he gets along here. If he's maybe got a new career as a bronc."

"I thought so too."

"Hardly see him no more and when I do, he seems down in the mouth, but surely that don't mean he's mental."

"No, not mental like crazy, but he has been diagnosed with bipolar personality disorder. Sometimes it's called manic-depressive. He's supposed to take pills to manage it, but he quit them a while ago. Never told me about it. The physical therapist mentioned it the other day, assuming I knew."

"Bipolar, eh? And you never knew he had pills?"

"No. I don't think he's had any, not since we moved in together, anyway."

"Is it a big deal?"

"Yes."

"Maybe he's embarrassed."

"Could be, I suppose. Broken bones or cancer, people feel sorry for you. Depressed? Everyone thinks you're weak and you should snap out of it. I guess I can see why he'd be reluctant to tell me, at first anyway. But besides that, sometimes he's downright obnoxious. He wasn't like this in Katawasis Lake, or believe me, I never would have hooked up with him. But the worst thing is that I think his attitude is preventing him from getting better. And I don't know what to do."

"Hmmm. He ain't getting better, feels shitty 'bout that, so he don't get better."

"That's about the size of it."

"Well, I dunno what can be done about that, other than to get him back on his pills."

"You ever tried to get a cat to swallow a pill? That would be easier."

"Maybe Stu can persuade him." She lifts her chin in the direction of the chute, where Felix has settled onto Rocky. "Here we go," she says.

When Felix nods, the gate is pulled open. Horse and rider catapult out. I've seen Rocky buck, but I never realized how far off the ground he could leap. Two jumps out of the chute and he does exactly what he did to K.C.: he rears, spins, leaps, plants his front hooves and drops his shoulder while simultaneously scooting sideways. Felix goes off the same way K.C. did. He gets up immediately, turns and waves to the crowd.

Red blows out a long breath and says, "Thank the Creator."

"K.C. will be happy to learn a champion bronc rider couldn't stick through that," I say. "I think we just found Rocky's place in the world. I doubt that was that was even five seconds."

I'm started by a man's voice close behind me. "Looks like that big black horse of yours will make a good bucking horse."

I turn to see one of Trina's friends. He grins and says, "I hear good bucking horses are worth a lot. Too bad he ain't healthy."

"What are you talking about?"

He doesn't reply, just grins, turns and saunters away.

Although it's a warm Indian summer day, a shiver courses through me.

K.C. won't leave the house even to go over to the Pedersen's, so Red, Stu and the boys are having dinner with us. I'm an indifferent cook at best. My go-to dish for company is roast chicken, but I spent most of the afternoon at the Rocking R, so Stu brought a couple of barbequed fryers from the Bistro. I boiled garden-fresh potatoes in their jackets and corn on the cob. Red contributed her famous leaf-lettuce-with-sugar-sweet-sour-cream-dressing salad.

"Jeez, K.C., you should've seen Rocky," Charlie says. "First we didn't expect he'd even buck, he was so quiet in the chute."

"Like a regular saddle horse," Johnny adds.

"Yeah, quiet like that," Charlie agrees. "Then he come out of the chute like a bat outta hell. He's going to be our star bucking horse. Going to make us some big bucks, Felix says."

"Sure. As long as he doesn't decide two seconds out of the chute that he'd rather be a dressage horse and just piaffes away," K.C. says.

"What's piaffes?" Johnny asks.

"K.C.'s joking," Stu replies. "Pass them spuds, please."

I push the bowl of potatoes into Stu's reach, and say, "So, guys, you probably didn't notice, but some of the bikers came over to watch."

"Did they, now?" Stu says.

"Uh-huh. And the one that was in my face at the rodeo was standing right behind me when Felix's ride was over."

"He didn't do nothing to you, did he, Auntie?" Charlie asks.

"No. But what he said has me worried."

"Trust you to find something to worry about," K.C. says.

"What did he say?" Stu asks.

"He said it looks like Rocky—well, he called him the black horse—is going to make a good bucking horse. He says he's heard they're worth something. And it's too bad he's not healthy."

"I think we'd know better'n that asshole if a horse is healthy," Stu says.

"That's what I thought, too," I say.

"No big deal. Just a smart ass know-nothing shooting his mouth off," Charlie says.

Everyone seems to agree with Charlie. Am I the only one who thinks it was a threat?

The next morning, I'm in my office, clearing up odds and ends. Being Monday, the Bistro is closed, so I'm not needed there. K.C. comes thumping down the hall on his crutches, holds up in the doorway and asks, "You going to town today?"

"If I can clear up a few rats and mice I'll be done for the day. We can go to town then, if you like."

"I didn't say I wanted to go. I just asked if you're going."

"Okay then, no, I have no plans to go to town. But maybe we could go grab lunch at Billie's. Nice change of scenery. Maybe see if Carol and Fred will meet us there? They were asking about you when I saw them over at the Rocking R yesterday."

"You really think I feel like socializing, especially in that biker's bar you've always said was too redneck for you?"

"Well, why go there when we have the Bistro? But I thought it would be good to get away for a change and it's closer for Carol and Fred—"

"I'm nearly out of Oxy and my gut's giving me hell. You need to go to the drug store."

"Tell you what, sweetie. I'll go, but not without you. We don't have to stop at Billie's, but—"

Before I finish my sentence, he turns and thumps away. I call after him, "K.C.! If not Billie's, how about we take a run into Swift Current for an early dinner at the Pioneer House? You could have your favorite baby back ribs."

"I told you, I'm not going anywhere. My gut's too sore," he calls back over his shoulder.

So much for my hope we could do something together. I thought time together, away from Wacasko-Wâti, might be what our relationship needs, but if he won't even budge for baby back ribs, what chance do I have?

I exhale a long breath and slump back in my chair. I'm thinking of going to the kitchen to top up my coffee, when I glance out the window over my desk and see Stu standing in the middle of the parking lot. That's odd. He'd usually be walking purposefully on his way somewhere, but he seems to have stalled out, coffee mug in hand, staring into space. Lately, he's been having frequent what he calls senior's moments. It's easy to chuckle and put it down to natural aging, but just standing in the yard looking lost seems more serious than that.

I top up my coffee and go to join him. Henry even gets up from his doggie bed on the porch and limps along with me. When I reach him, I say, "Hey, Stu."

"Oh, hi, Lindy," he says. He scratches Henry's ear, but barely glances my way.

"Nice morning," I comment.

"Ay-yuh," he agrees. Only now does he face me, his expression perplexed as if he doesn't know how he got here. He turns away again and I look out across the road to see what he's so focused on. Nothing interesting there as far as I can tell.

"What's up?"

"I, er, dunno. I think I was going to do something, but now I can't remember what it was. Guess I'll have to go back to where I started before I can remember." He pats his shirt pocket and finding no Copenhagen there, chuckles and says, "Damn! Forgot I quit the snoose, too.

"Yeah, I don't know how many times I've gone into the kitchen and then can't remember what I went there for. But I've never tried snoose, or if I did, I've forgotten." I chuckle.

Stu doesn't react to my lame attempt at humor and makes no move to go anywhere, as if he'll remember where he was going if he waits long enough. Then he looks at me and with a grin, he's back to the Stu I know. Relieved, I ask, "So, what were you so interested in over at the road just now?"

"The birds," he replies, and points at the sky. "Them, whaddayacall 'em, turkey vultures."

Now I realize he wasn't looking out at the road, but at the sky far off, where there are half a dozen vultures, not much more than dots, circling one of the Rocking R's distant pastures. Stu may have forgotten his mission, but there's nothing wrong with his distance vision.

"Looks like something's dead," I comment. "Another cougar kill? We still got the late calvers over there?"

"Naw, we moved 'em up into the home pasture last week. But something's dead over there, that's for sure. Want to ride out with me and see what it is? If you're too busy, it could wait 'til the boys get home from school."

"Nope, I've got time right now and I'd love to ride."

"Me too. I'll get Shorty and Chica, if you haul out the saddles," he offers.

"Deal," I agree. I don't tell him I'm happy for any excuse to get away because my last exchange with K.C. would be enough to drag anyone's mood down, and riding is good for the soul. I go into the tack room to get the saddles, then wonder if K.C. could be convinced to come with us. I'll offer to saddle his horse and bring him right up to the steps so all he'd have to do would be to ditch the crutches and climb on. It would be good for his mood. Instead of running up to the house to ask, I pick up the phone and call, thinking I might have to let it ring a while because of how long it takes him to get to it. But the line is busy. I pack our saddles out to the stands near the crossties, and when I go back into the tack room for the bridles, try phoning the house again. Same result. I give up.

Horses tacked up, we mount, ride up the driveway and then in the ditch as far as the new entrance to the Rocking R. We go through the barnyard, past the corrals and into the pasture. Stu is his old self, the sweet guy I remember from way back when I first met him and my father, and it's easy to understand why Red was attracted to him. The north breeze is brisk as usual at this time of year, but the sun is warm. The air is fresh, and the only sounds are the squeaking of the tack, birdsong, and the odd far-off moo or whinny. I'm reminded I'm fortunate to be here.

"We should do this more often," I say.

"Ay-yuh," Stu agrees. "Wisht Red liked it more. Not that I ain't enjoying riding with you."

"I know. I wish K.C. was with us, too. Would do him a world of good."

"Maybe a little far for his first time back in the saddle, but you're goddamn right 'bout that. Tried to talk to him like you gals wanted, but it didn't go nowhere."

"Head like a rock, that one," I say, and click my tongue. With a lift of my chin to indicate the circling vultures, I ask, "You think we're getting close?"

"Should be," Stu says.

"I think we're going to come to the end of our property pretty quick. Maybe the new bison ranch lost a calf."

"Don't want to wish 'em any ill luck, but I sure hope it's one of theirs and not one of ours."

"At least you and I—" My train of thought is interrupted by what we see as we come to the crest of the hill. A short distance away, definitely still on our property, half a dozen vultures flutter around a black mound on the ground.

We spur our horses into a canter and chase the vultures off.
This is no cougar kill.

# Chapter 9

Late afternoon a few days later, an RCMP cruiser rolls in, parks at the Bistro, and Sgt. Coleman gets out. I go to the entrance to greet him.

"Hi, Lindy," he says, "got a minute?"

"Absolutely," I say, "I'll fetch Stu. Meanwhile, grab a mug there and help yourself to coffee. Wanna try one of our world-famous cinnamon buns? On the house!"

"Um, sure."

"I'll get Marcie to bring you one. Go ahead and join K.C. over there." I point across the floor to where K.C. sits at the fireplace, back to the room, crutches leaning against the masonry, his dark scowl a result of my refusal to bring anything up to the house for his lunch. I suppose he didn't choose a seat at the staff table to make sure we all knew he was mad, but at least he's not holed up in the house, and if that's what it takes to get him out, I'm willing to let him be mad.

"And K.C. is...?"

"Oh, you haven't met him yet. He's my boyfriend. Go and introduce yourself. I'll be back in a flash and join you there."

"Okay," he says, and heads for the coffee bar. In the kitchen, I ask Marcie to get Sgt. Coleman a cinnamon bun, then go out to the barn.

Stu is at the far end of the alleyway next to the AMT, talking to Johnny, who's inside the stall, picking manure and tossing it into the box of the little vehicle. "Hey, Stu," I call out, "Sergeant Coleman is here. Come and join us for a coffee."

"Ay-yuh," he says. "Be right there."

By the time I'm back in the Bistro, Red is sitting with K.C. and Sgt. Coleman. Stu and I join them.

"So, Sergeant Coleman, have you got news?" I ask. It would be nice to be on a first-name basis as we were with Dwight, but he doesn't suggest it.

"You been to the Rocking R?" Stu asks.

"I have. Actually, been there a couple times," he replies, and butters a section of his cinnamon bun. "Have to, or Felix wouldn't quit bugging me. He's pretty steamed about that horse."

An innocent statement, maybe, but the way he said it makes me think it's a criticism. "Can't blame him, can you?" I ask. I struggle to keep my tone neutral when I add, "We're all pretty *steamed*. The flood was bad enough, but to kill a beautiful horse to get at us?"

K.C. says, "You never liked that horse, Lindy, so don't pretend you're sorry he's dead."

I draw a quick breath. To avoid snarling at him, I get up and go to the bar to get a glass of wine. By the time I come back to the table, I've mostly gotten my anger under control. Still, instead of returning to my chair beside K.C., I stand leaning back against the fireplace, holding my glass in unsteady hands.

While I was away from the table, Sgt. Coleman must have told the others about meeting with Trina. He says, "She reminded us that we seized all their guns when her husband was arrested."

"Ain't like any of 'em couldn't of bought a gun since then," Red points out.

"Besides, you got Russ put away, but he didn't act alone," I add. "And everyone around here has a rifle. At least a .22. They wouldn't have to buy one. They could just steal—"

Before I finish my sentence, Sgt. Coleman says, "Anyway, as expected, Trina claims to know nothing about your irrigation being sabotaged or the horse being shot, and without any evidence, there's no way to prove otherwise. She gave me names and contact info for half a dozen other fellas, and we'll interview them, but don't hold your breath. They'll never admit anything. And the horse wasn't shot with a .22. Game Warden says most likely a thirty-aught-six. Something a hunter would use. So, he was shot by accident."

"Goddammit!" Stu exclaims. "Shot by accident?! He was twice the size of a deer and black to boot."

"Do you think a deer hunter could accidentally shoot him right between the eyes?" I ask.

"It happened overnight, right? So, they had to be pit-lamping," Sgt. Coleman says. "All they'd see was eyes, so it makes sense that's where he'd be shot."

"A long ways from the road for pit-lampers. Besides, it wasn't necessarily overnight," I argue. "The rodeo ended at four, which would give them more than three hours of daylight. Easy to drive into the pasture to find the herd and shoot him. The horses aren't afraid of people or vehicles, so they wouldn't run. He wouldn't have to shoot him from hundreds of yards away, he could walk right up to him. Do you think it's a coincidence that this particular horse, one they said wasn't healthy out of a herd of dozens, ends up dead the next morning?"

Sgt. Coleman frowns before continuing, "Conservation has their game wardens on it. We have no reason to believe anyone at the Rocking R was involved." He turns his attention to polishing off his cinnamon bun.

"But the threat..." I let my sentence trail off as I realize as threats go, saying the horse looked unhealthy is pretty vague. I take a sip of wine and say nothing more.

A hush falls over the group. Finally, Stu asks, "Anything more about that li'l gal Janey? Or the other missing gal?"

"Nothing new," Sgt. Coleman replies, then finishes chewing before continuing, "we've had a few dozen tips in response to our press conference. Investigated those that sounded legit, but nothing's gone anywhere."

Now my curiosity is aroused. "Tips? Like what?"

"Reports of a guy in a truck hanging around the Husky where Janey's mom works. If anyone had been able to describe the truck or the guy in it, maybe. Some said a brown or black pickup. Maybe a Chevy or maybe a Ford. But just a truck like thousands of others, at a truck stop? Not enough to go on."

"You ain't going to give up, are you?" Red wants to know.

"Never. Major Crimes won't close the file until they find the guy."

"But they've got hundreds of cold cases, right?" I ask. "So, the file might not be closed, but for all the investigating that's going on, it might as well be."

Sgt. Coleman responds with a shrug. His frown tells me we're not going to be buddies like we were with Dwight. "Well," he says, and gets to his feet, "thanks for the coffee."

"Good to see you, Sergeant," I say, hoping there's no sarcastic tone in my voice. "Drop in any time."

Everyone says their goodbyes. Red starts bussing the table and waves off my help, so I head up to my house to get a start on payroll for tomorrow, but can't focus because of runaway imaginings of the Rocking R pickup with bikers in the box, bouncing across the pasture, coming to a stop near the horse herd, and the guy with the gray stripes in his beard shooting Rocky without even getting out.

I close down the computer, go into the kitchen and start a pot of chili, which does nothing to stop the mental images of Rocky landing on the ground with a *whump!* When I have everything in the pot and it's starting to simmer, I head for the armchair in the living room, flip on the TV, but find nothing I want to watch. I tune it to MTV and pick up the book on the end table: *A Prayer for Owen Meany*, a new release I bought a few weeks ago and haven't even opened yet. Thankfully between it and the background music, the sickening mental images stop and I forget everything but the story. Until the smoke detector screeches. I hurry to turn off the stove, grab a tea towel and flap it at the smoke detector until it quits. I'm stirring the chili vigorously, hoping the burnt bits I'm scraping off the bottom won't be noticeable once they're mixed in, when K.C. comes in.

"How does it feel to be out and about again?" I ask.

"I'd be happier if we had something decent for dinner."

"It's just a little scorched. I think I caught it in time," I reply, knowing full well I hadn't. "I was going to make cornbread to go with it, but kind of lost track of the time. I can still make it, if you're okay with waiting half an hour." As I'm getting a bowl and the cornbread mix out, I say, "I thought you were coming up right behind me."

"Darlene was just driving in, so I went to talk to her."

"Oh, Darlene's here? That's right. She said she had a friend who'd like to come for lessons. Is that who you called?"

"Who I called? I didn't call anyone.

"I mean this morning."

"I said I didn't call anyone," he reiterates. "You know what? Forget the cornbread. I'll pass on the burnt chili and get something decent at the Bistro." He turns and hobbles back out the door. I flip him the bird, but since the door is already shut, he'll never know it.

The burnt bits are very noticeable in the chili, and the whole batch is ruined. Despite that, I make myself some garlic toast and heap a spoonful of chili on it for every bite. I could go down to the Bistro, too, but I'm determined to eat the damned chili, telling myself it's not that bad. It *is* that bad, though. Oh, well. The dogs will eat it pretty much anything, so it's not a complete loss. I put the pot out on the porch and Henry gets up off his bed to come and sniff. He gives me an odd look as if he agrees with K.C. "You're damn fussy for a mutt anyone else would've shot by now. Eat it, or no treats for you," I warn. He licks his lips and gives his tail a weak twitch, but doesn't hazard a taste. "No flies on you, buddy," I say, and scratch his ears. Red and Stu's dogs aren't that fussy and frequently check my porch to see what Henry has turned his nose up at, so the pot will be licked clean before long.

When I've eaten a bowl of Cheerios and start cleaning up the kitchen, my thoughts turn to Wacasko-Wâti finances. If K.C. isn't able to train or coach, am I willing to support him? The roller coaster ride of living with his moods is becoming unbearable, but until half an hour ago, when he denied making a phone call when I know he did, I wasn't sure of the answer. Now that I know how easily he can lie to me, it's clear.

# Chapter 10

M y friend Kristy's husband Jim is an ex-cop, current fraud investigator for Western Savings & Loan. I met him when I was working at the WS&L branch in Katawasis Lake. He'd been sent to investigate some funny business at the branch, met my roommate Kristy, and they've been a couple ever since. They're still my friends even though we don't see each other more than a few times a year.

Jim is an ace lock-picker, a skill I admired, so he gave me a set of lock pick tools to thank me for my help. Or maybe as a joke, never expecting me to use them. I'm not sure which. I'll have to ask him sometime. When I got into the P.I. thing, he advised me to pay for a membership in Identi-Co. Among other things, they provide reverse phone number look-ups. Invaluable in cheating husband cases. Never thought I'd have to use it for that myself.

K.C. had to know I'd notice all the long distance calls to the same number. Maybe he thought I wouldn't know who the number belonged to. Ordinarily I wouldn't, but I have Identi-Co.! Which turns out not to be any help at all. The number is unlisted. At some point I suppose I'll have to ask him about it. I know he'll either lie or flip out, so instead I avoid the issue by spending more time away.

Even though I've told myself at least a thousand times that it's stupid, anytime I'm near Swift Current, I make the side trip to Dogpatch. Today, I have an eight p.m. appointment, an assignment from SGI to interview a witness. Evening appointments are the downside to the job. It only takes an hour or so to get a statement, complete with a sketch of which vehicles were where, so it's easy money, but these task assignments are always with people that refuse to come to SGI's office. It's a case of setting up an appointment when it suits them, which is usually inconvenient for me. Now I'm happy for anything that takes me away, even if it means I won't be home until late. Today, I'm half an hour ahead of schedule. Just enough time, if I'm quick.

I've just turned onto the street that leads to the railroad crossing when BBB's truck passes me heading in the opposite direction. I almost didn't recognize it in the low light, and I probably would have missed it if he hadn't passed me where there are street lights. I count myself lucky he did, because if he'd been in Dogpatch, he would have wondered about a vehicle coming down his street that late and may have confronted me again. In our many discussions, Jim said being a successful investigator is five percent follow your nose, and ninety-five percent luck. I was in luck tonight.

There's no electricity at the house, so it's odd he would be there this late. It's almost dark, and with all the windows boarded up, it would be impossible to work inside the house. Besides, he's always left in time to get home for dinner. But the important thing is that it's unlikely he'll be back tonight. I drive to the end of the street and around to the back lane where I conceal my truck in the caragana bushes. After a few minutes of watching to make sure he hasn't doubled back, I hoof it up the lane. No use checking out the house, because although I could pick the lock on the front door, this time I'm more interested in the shed.

The shed has an overhead door on the lane. On the off chance it's not locked, I twist the handle and wrench on it, but something's stopping it from rolling up. I go around the outhouse to the man door, hold my flashlight in my teeth and get to work on the padlock. It's a good one, and it takes me a while to cheat it. Just when I'm about to give up, it springs open. I glance around to make sure the area is still deserted, then remove the lock, fold the hasp back, push the door open just far enough to shine the flashlight in, and see—nothing.

Nothing, that is, except the rubble of decades. A rusted bicycle chain on the battered work bench. Anemic-looking weeds pushing through a loose board. A dark area in the crumbling concrete floor where who knows how many vehicles have leaked oil over the years. An untidy heap of kerosene cans in the far corner. Nothing to indicate the shed's been used for anything in decades. The reason I couldn't open the overhead door? A padlock through the holes in the rail blocks the rollers. Why bother locking this up? Is he worried someone would steal those cans?

If I tell anyone how much trouble I went to just to see the inside of this old shed, they'll think I'm delusional, brain dead, or both, and I'm starting to think they'd be right. I promise myself I won't waste any more mental energy thinking about Dogpatch and BBB and won't come here again. I push the door shut and I'm about to close the padlock when I realize there was something I should have paid more attention to: something white near the wall. Too bright and clean to belong here.

I open the door again and slip inside. The white object is a piece of paper. Just as I'm picking it up, I hear a vehicle. I've never known BBB to come here twice in one day, but there's a first time for everything. I shove the paper in my pocket and hurry out, flicking my flashlight off and pulling the door shut behind me. I hustle around the outhouse to the lane. I poke my head around the corner of the garage, and see not one vehicle, but two, side by side on the street, facing back toward town. The engines chortle as the drivers rev them. Male voices yell back and forth. It's a challenge. My heart gradually quits thumping.

Once I'm safely in my truck, I pull the paper out of my pocket. It's a ticket. There's what looks like a shoe print, as if someone stepped on it. The event? Last summer's Alice In Chains concert at the Minot Air Force Base. A grunge band? I followed Beer Belly Boy enough to know he's a country music fan.

So much for putting him out of my mind.

Once home, I pull the ticket out of my pocket before taking my jeans off and heaping them on the clothes hamper. What was I thinking? It's probably nothing. If the kids go there to drag race, maybe they used the shed to party, and that's why BBB put the locks on it. Sometimes following your nose is a fool's errand. I toss the ticket in the wastebasket. Then I don my jammies and climb into bed, careful to stick to my side so I don't wake K.C.

My eyes pop open. I look at the clock radio. Two a.m. Why am I awake? That ticket! I go into the ensuite and dig it out of the trash. Why didn't I leave it where it was and tell someone about it? Sgt. Coleman maybe? But even Stu's old buddy Dwight thought many of my suspicions were nuts, and we barely know Sgt. Coleman. He's such a by-the-booker he wouldn't do a thing. Anyway, no judge in the world would give him or the Swift Current cops a search warrant because some P.I. with barely a year's experience under her belt saw a piece of paper in an old garage.

I carefully stow the ticket in the box of tampons in the vanity. I'll decide what, if anything, to do with it some other time.

We had an appointment with the surgeon, who confirmed K.C. is healing and there's nothing amiss with any screws. Then, in a session with our family doctor, K.C. agreed to go back on his meds. He grumbles about brain fog. I'm glad he's back to normal. I can hardly believe I was so close to tossing him out not that long ago.

He's recovered enough that when we got our first big dump of snow, he ventured all the way down to the barn using only a couple of canes. He's gone down every day since, chatting with whoever happens to be there, whether it's one of the few remaining boarders, or Charlie and Johnny, who clean stalls and ride rescue horses after school.

One afternoon as I'm treating myself to a coffee break walk-about, I hear his voice in the tack room, and head into the barn. He's just coming out when I get to the door. "Hi," I say. "I heard your voice."

"Oh," he says, "I was on the phone." He looks at me and then away so quickly I nearly turn to see if there's someone coming up behind me. Then he continues, "Yeah, you know I've been um, I'm calling past boarders, to see if they want to come back now. And some other horse people. So, there's going to be a lot of long distance calls on the phone bill."

As if I hadn't noticed. But I don't tell him he's a little late telling me, and instead ask, "What's the response been?"

"Good. Yeah, I think we'll be back to normal pretty quick. If not right away, at least by January." He gives me the movie star smile that melted my heart back in Katawasis Lake and says,

"Well, I'm done in for today. Time to hit the recliner." He turns and hobbles away.

I'm flooded with empathy. Here he is, doing the best he can to get things running again, even though it takes so much out of him. He was seriously injured, and what do I do? Plan how to turf him out of his home. I promise myself to push his lie about his phone calls out of my head and be a better person going forward.

❦

This morning, I'm back in after turn-out duty and we're having coffee and a couple of yesterday's cinnamon buns, both of us on stools at the island. K.C. says, "I think I can book a few clinics here this winter."

"Good idea," I agree, "but it would mean teaching six or more lessons every day. Even if you sit for much of it, do you really feel up to that?"

"No, that would be too much, right now anyway. But I can get back into lessons a little at a time. I've been talking to the boarders we still have, and we're going to start lessons again. A few lessons a week isn't enough to do much good for my bottom line, though. The others I phoned, most of them will come back, but maybe not until January. Get an early start on gearing up for show season."

"Exactly," I agree, slide off my stool, and take my mug to the coffeemaker for a refill. "That's a big reason why they came here in the first place, right? I mean, that, and the fact you're here to coach them."

"Right. Only thing is, looking after a bunch more horses—not sure how much stall cleaning I can do. And it could be too much for the boys, what with school, plus the rescue horses need to be worked and it would take them away from that."

"We'll hire someone to clean stalls if we need to. Maybe Harry. He's laid off for the winter now, but he's mentioned he'd like to work in the barn. We have to get used to it. Felix isn't available much anymore, Stu's getting older and Charlie's off to Olds College next year." I lift the pot and ask, "Want a top up?"

"Yes, please," he replies, and holds up his cup. "And I didn't mean *I'd* do the clinics What I'm thinking is to have other clinicians, big name folks, come. We host it, charge enough to pay the clinician and make us a profit besides."

"Could we get enough interest to make that do-able?"

"If we book good trainers, sure. Folks would come from Alberta and Manitoba, I bet, if we got some big name cutting horse trainers. Maybe barrel racers. Reining. Colt starting. The whole kit and kaboodle." He heaves a sigh and smiles. "You were right. It feels good to be doing something again." He swivels his stool and picks at a thread on his cuff, then says, "Babe, I know I've been a real shit about the whole, um, bipolar thing. I want you to know I'm sorry, and um, thank you for putting up with my, er, for putting up with me."

"You're welcome, sweetie. What else could I do? I love you." As I say it, I realize it's true.

"I know. And I love you."

After I top up his mug and put the carafe back on the warming plate, I kiss him. Just a quick peck. Then he pulls me to him and makes it a good one.

It's been quite a while since I've wanted to kiss him. I hope that nice feeling sticks around. I'm feeling so kindly disposed toward him, I say, "Since your kids couldn't come at Thanksgiving, I was thinking maybe they could come on their next Professional Development Day. Charlie and Johnny have one the last Friday in October, so it's a long weekend. The school your kids go to likely does, too. If we went and picked them up on the night before, that would make three full days here."

"Um, sure." He glances at his watch and says, "I saw Ester's truck come in a while ago. She must be on the horse by now. I'm going to go watch for a bit." He slides off the stool, organizes his canes, then heads out the door.

"Can I leave it with you, then?" I call after him. The door closes and I don't know if he heard.

# Chapter 11

Late October, school P.D. day behind us, and no mention from K.C. of his kids coming for a visit. When I asked him about it, he said he didn't have time, what with organizing the clinic.

Today, Charlie and Johnny are putting up advertisers' banners, currently on ladders erecting the ten-foot-long vinyl Maple Creek Chrysler Dodge banner. K.C. is supervising. We've moved our round pen in from outside and rented enough extra pipe panels to cordon off the audience area. Felix and Stu are working on that. We've rented a hundred chairs and are just waiting for them to be delivered. Will we really need that many? Will people drive out this far just to audit? Time will tell.

This will be the first-ever Wacasko-Wâti Cowboy Challenge. We're using our own rescue horses—those no more than halter-broke—and each of the four competitors will draw a horse. They'll work with it Friday, Saturday, and Sunday and hopefully will be riding them at walk, trot and canter—extra points for being on the correct lead—by the end. A couple of other well-known cowboys are judges. All four contestants will keep their project horses. The winner also gets a one-year lease on a brand new Ram three-quarter ton dually courtesy of Maple Creek Chrysler Dodge, and a check for $1,000 thanks to Wacasko-Wâti. K.C. assures me the sponsors he lined up coupled with increased Bistro and wine sales will more than cover it. We've been experiencing an uptick in customers for days, so excitement seems to be building. He may be right. Fingers crossed we don't get any more snow.

Things are rolling along so well that K.C. is elated. So elated, I wonder if he's off his meds again. I'd ask him, but he'd resent being questioned. Maybe I should count his pills. Too sneaky? Better to be upfront and ask. I'll put it off until the end of the month, when he should be needing more. Although... Would he flush his meds to make sure he ran out on schedule? That's what I would do if I was him. But he's not me. Being a suspicious person, while a great asset for a P.I., can have a serious downside in a relationship.

I'm pondering this while standing in the doorway watching the goings-on. The hiss of jake brakes interrupts my thoughts and I turn to see the A-1 Septic flatbed truck with a couple of porta-potties on board turning in. There's a men's and ladies' washroom in the Bistro as well as a unisex one in the barn, but our septic system isn't set up for crowds, so we rented porta-potties just in case we actually get crowds. I head out to tell the driver where we want them, but K.C. passes me, barely using his canes. Getting back to work has definitely been good for him, but practically running? Now I really think I need to count pills.

Instead of returning to the indoor arena, I go to the Bistro for something to eat while I'm waiting for Kristy to arrive. I'm starting on my hungry cowhand-size bowl of beef barley soup and two thick slices of salt rising bread when I see Kristy's little red Fiero drive in and go up to park in my driveway. I go to the door and step outside to call and let her know where I am, just as Mark's truck comes in and parks near the Bistro entrance. The man in question gets out, but although he glances my way, he doesn't see me. Why not? Because he's gawking at Kristy, who is out of her car and looking my way. Kristy, with her Liz Taylor good looks and curvy little body, is a head-turner even in jeans and a ski jacket, even at this distance. She smiles, and waves. If Mark thinks she's waving at him, he might already be getting a chubby. He's a red-blooded male, after all. I save him potential embarrassment by saying, "Hey, Mark! You're just in time to meet my friend."

He looks my way, notices me at last, and says, "Oh, hi, Lindy."

"She's here for the weekend. To help out in case we're really busy, you know, with the Challenge and all."

"Oh yeah? Well, whaddaya know, I'm here to volunteer, too."

"What a coincidence," I say, and wonder if he only made the decision when he saw Kristy and learned she'd be here for the weekend. "Get yourself a coffee and whatever, and go sit at the staff table. The guys are pretty busy in the ring and will be glad for your help, if you're planning on going to work right away. I'm going up to get Kristy settled in her room and we'll be down to join you in a few minutes." I turn and hustle across the parking lot to where Kristy is waiting.

"Hey, girlfriend!" I say. "Great to see you!" We both grab luggage and head into the house. "Glad you came early," I tell her as I put her suitcase on the bed in the spare room. "Any trouble on the drive?"

"Nope, all good. The only trouble was ignoring Jim's grouchy face when I wouldn't have sex with him before I left this morning. Like, he's already late for work, I'm anxious to get going, and he wants a quickie. I could barely get his paws off me. I don't know how many times he made remarks about all the cowboys that would be here this weekend, and how he doubts their wives will be with them. So, I think he just wanted sex to remind me I'm his wife. Or to make sure I wasn't horny when I got here. Like a quickie with him would do anything about that! Typical man. He has an inflated opinion of his—"

"Yeah, typical," I interrupt. Her marriage has ups and downs just like mine, only not because either of them is bi-polar. Kristy thinks being faithful means she can do as she wishes as long as she goes back to her husband. She claims Jim is welcome to do likewise and is good with it. I'm not so sure about that, but I think if he made waves, he might lose her, and he's still thoroughly smitten. I can't help thinking how different our lives would be if Jim and I had hooked up. I was attracted to him from the first time I met him, and although K.C. and I had dated by that time, it was far from a committed relationship. But Kristy scooped him up, and I ended up with K.C. Not that K.C. was the consolation prize. Far from it. I was pretty stoked about it at the time. I love K.C. and Jim wouldn't fit in at the ranch like K.C. does, if he would even want to live here, so it's better this way. Or so I tell myself.

"He could've come with me," Kristy continues. "Wouldn't kill him to tell Pissy she has to keep the kids this weekend even though it's his turn. Right?"

"I guess not," I agree. I could tell her she's lucky Priscilla, AKA Pissy, lets him have as much time with the kids as she does, or like K.C., Jim might want her to have a baby, and I doubt she's changed her mind about not having kids. "Well anyway, come and have lunch. You better eat, because we might have to put you to work ahead of schedule."

"Already getting that busy?"

"Yeah. Surprisingly, we've had more than the usual number of customers in the last week or so. Advertising the Cowboy Challenge seems to be creating spinoff. Lots of non-horse people have been showing up. But besides that, one of my old friends from college is here. I'll introduce you."

"*That's* the guy you were just talking to? This is going to be a *fu-uh-un* week!"

I sigh. Poor Jim! He's about to be forgotten, at least short term. I resign myself to having Kristy around longer than planned. Judging by the multiple suitcases and garbage bags stuffed with her belongings heaped on the passenger seat and filling every nook and cranny in her tiny car, that may have been her plan all along. I'm happy for her to stay as long as she wants, but I wish her marriage was in better shape, for both their sakes. "Take as long as you want to settle in. I'm just having a bowl of soup, but I'll be back up pretty quick. If you're hungry, come down to the Bistro," I say.

"I've been thinking about your cinnamon buns for the last hour. I'll be there in five minutes," she agrees. "I'll just fix my makeup and come down."

Kristy has never been able to fix her makeup in five minutes, so maybe Mark will have gone to talk to K.C. about volunteering by the time she comes down. With luck, their paths won't cross all weekend. I hope that's the case, knowing it's unlikely. But whatever happens, happens.

Back in the Bistro, I find Mark with a beer in front of him, settled at the staff table across from my rapidly cooling soup. I barely sit down when he asks, "So your friend. What's her story?"

"Well, I met her when I lived in Katawasis Lake. She worked at the local pub so she's great help around here, doesn't even need training. I rented a basement suite. She and her second husband lived upstairs, and we ended up being roommates when they split. Now she's living with her third husband, in Calgary." Why all the detail? Maybe I want to get it across to Mark that she's married and that she's a heartbreaker. Although instead of warning him off, it may have given him the idea that she may be married, but that isn't necessarily a roadblock to a relationship, or at least a fling.

"So, how's her present marriage going?"

"Um, well, fine, I think. Why?"

He shrugs and says, "Just making conversation." He gives me a grin and a wink. If he hadn't done that, I may have believed he truly was *just making conversation.* "Here's my food." With a lift of his chin he indicates Marcie, coming our way with his burger. She sets it in front of him. "Thanks, Marcie," he says.

"You bet," she replies. "Need anything else?"

"No, I'm good, thanks."

After what had to be the quickest makeup fix of her life, Kristy comes into the Bistro. How do busty women manage to find low cut T-shirts when the rest of us have to settle for those that come up to our chins? I've always told myself big boobs just get in the way when you're shooting pool, so I'm happy the way I am. Not that I've ever played pool. Anyway, Mark follows her with his eyes as she goes to the pastry counter and asks Marcie to warm up a cinnamon bun. She smiles at us as she fills a mug of coffee at the self-serve coffee bar, then comes to take the chair next to me.

"Kristy, this is Mark, a friend from college," I say. "Mark, meet my good friend, Kristy."

They exchange their hellos and pleased-to-meet-yous and from that point on, I might as well not be here. I finish my lunch and I'm about to excuse myself just in case they'd actually notice my leaving, when a customer hurries out of the washroom and goes to the cashier desk, asking for the owner or manager loudly enough to be heard by pretty well everyone in the place. Marcie waves at me and I go to see what it's about.

Rather than appearing angry over some Bistro problem, the young woman looks worried.

"Is something wrong?" I ask.

"Yeah, well, um, the toilet is overflowing," she responds. "I didn't put anything down it, honest. Just, when I flushed, the water rose instead of going down. I flushed again, in case, you know... Anyway, then it went right over the top."

"Want me to get K.C. or Stu?" Marcie asks.

"No, it's okay. I'll get the plunger and take care of it," I tell her.

"It wasn't my fault," the young woman says.

"I know," I assure her, "it happens. It's okay." Yeah, it happens all right, too often. Why don't people pay attention to the sign that says nothing but poop, pee, and toilet paper are supposed to be flushed? Surely women are smart enough to figure out what the little bin next to the toilet is for.

I give her a smile and a nod, and head into the back, destination janitor's closet, to get the plunger, rolling bucket, and mop. When I go through to the back hall, there's already water on the floor. That's more than a little overflow. What I see when I open the door causes my hope of clearing it with a plunger to die. This is more than one plugged toilet. I back out and position the bucket and mop to block the Bistro entrance to the hall, poke my head into the kitchen and ask Lucy to put out the yellow warning cones and make "out of order" signs for the bathrooms, redirecting them to the porta potties or the bathroom in the tack room. "No more water down the drain unless there's no alternative," I tell them. "Red, help me mop please."

We're mopping vigorously to keep ahead of the flood until A-1 Septic comes to pump the tank, when Johnny comes running in. "Mom! The toilet in the tack room is overflowing. Dad said to—" He stops up at the wet floor cone and realizes what we're doing. "Here, too?" he asks.

"Yeah, here, too," I respond. So much for customers using the toilet in the tack room.

"If you ain't needed back at the barn, get busy here," Red says, and hands him the mop. Just then, there's a scream, or more of a loud squeak, from the kitchen. She hustles away to check it out. I lean my mop against the wall and follow.

We find Marcie, backed up as far as possible against the prep table, pointing at the floor next to where Red and I are standing. There's a case of chicken on the floor there, on top of the floor drain, preventing the flood water that's now flowing unchecked from the hall and into the kitchen, from draining. Between that and the counter is a dead rat.

"It's okay, Marcie," I say. "It's dead." I go for a dustpan to scoop it up, but Red dives past me, picks it up by the tail, and tosses it out the back door.

"Okay, crew," Red says, "Let's give the place a good going over and make goddamn sure there's no more surprises."

"How'd it get in here?" I ask.

"My fault, I guess," Barney says. "I guess it could run in because I sometimes prop the door open when I have a bunch of stuff to take in or out. Or if it's too hot."

"Well, that one's running days are long over," Red points out.

"Maybe Paisley Cat brought it in. You know, like a present. She likes to come in for a visit," Marcie suggests.

"Also my fault," Barney admits. "I like the company, 'specially when it's early and I'm working alone."

"He gives her chicken trimmings," Marcie explains.

"Well, that has to stop. The health department could shut us down for that, Barney," I say.

"I know, Boss. I'm sorry. It's just that Paisley Cat is so cute."

What do you know, the big galoot with hands the size of catcher's mitts and so much testosterone his chest and back hair forms a fringe at the neck opening of his chef's coat, is a cat person. "I know," I tell him. "You can still give her the trimmings, but somewhere away from the Bistro so it doesn't attract rats. Okay?"

He nods and says, "Sorry, boss."

"Okay," I say. "But the case of chicken on the floor? What possible reason is there for that? Red? You've been in here most of the morning. Didn't you notice?"

"If I did, it didn't hit home. Too busy, what with all the customers."

"Well, who put it there in the first place?" The entire staff, Barney, Marcie, Lucy, Red, and the two part-timers stand facing me.

"It was on the counter," Marcie says. "I don't know how it ended up on the floor."

I suppose the guilty party won't own up, and I guess I can't blame them. "Well, it's a mystery, then. And another violation. Just lucky we didn't get a surprise inspection. Make sure not to do it even if it's only for a couple of minutes, because it's easy to get busy and forget it's there. And everyone, be alert. Food doesn't go on the floor, even if it's in a box. All right?"

They all mutter agreement and return to their tasks. I return to the flood zone, which has grown in my absence. Red joins me and I send Johnny to get Stu to help us. Much more important to keep the overflow out of the food service area than anywhere it might go in the barn.

When I ordered porta-potties for the weekend, I didn't have Bistro customers in mind.

"I don't understand. How did this happen? We've had the tanks pumped on schedule, no problem," I say.

The Bistro is closed for the day. Red, Stu, K.C. and I are at the biggest table in the Bistro. Mark and Kristy are at an adjoining table. Stu has scotch neat while the rest of us are either drinking beer or wine. Brad, the owner of A-1 Septic and long-time friend of ours, came to take a look at what his crew was doing and is having a beer while updating us. "Looks like more than one issue," he says. "I think someone has been using a lot of bleach, because the system isn't cooking like it should. You use bleach in your kitchen?"

"Of course. You know that. We have to do a bleach rinse for dishes. We'd be shut down if we didn't. We thought we solved that problem by keeping the water from the bleach rinse separate from the septic system. It goes into that tank behind the building, and we use it for irrigation."

"Sensible," Brad agrees. "But there's also a major soft blockage, and we pulled out some diapers."

"Diapers?"

"Some of your customers must've flushed them. Not sure yet what the rest of the blockage is. Could be cat litter. You know, the so-called flushable kind. We'll have to dig up the lines if we can't get it cleared."

"But for both tanks? The Bistro *and* the barn? Bistro customers don't use the washroom in the barn."

"But they could, right?"

"But I doubt they'd change a baby there. They'd have to lay it on the concrete floor, and with workers coming in and out all the time, it's none too clean. And we don't have litter boxes. Our cats all go outside."

"Well, maybe it's not cat litter, then, but it's some kind of mush we don't see often. And more than one person has flushed diapers."

"Damn!" I sigh. "How long will it take to get everything back up and running?"

"Not that long. We'll get the backhoe here PDQ and we can start first thing in the morning. Unfortunately, in these low temperatures, it'll take a while for the solvent cement to cure."

"How long is a while?" K.C. asks.

"No way of knowing," Brad replies. "With luck, we'll have everything fixed and tested by Sunday. Monday at the latest."

"Great. Our busiest weekend of the entire year, and the washrooms are out of commission," I grumble. I get to my feet. "Is Felix still here, Stu?"

"Doubt it," Stu replies. "Why?"

"We need him to go and talk to Sergeant Coleman. I just figured out why we've had so many customers this week and I think I know who's behind it."

"I imagine you're going to blame Trina's crew," K.C. says.

"Of course, Trina's crew. So many women with little kids. I thought we'd just suddenly become a family destination. Kids loving the country experience, seeing the horses and so on. I even thought maybe next spring we should get a few goats and a potbellied pig and make it a proper kid experience. What a sucker! Now I realize those toddlers were just props, you know, to explain the diaper bags."

"You think this was deliberate?" Brad asks. "In that case... Well, maybe they know about powdered bleach. It's a concentrate, like sugar. Easy to dump into the toilet. But once it hits liquid, look out! Two cups of concentrate makes sixty gallons of bleach. Enough to kill all the bacteria and enzymes in the tank. They wouldn't need to flush diapers. Unless they were worried your systems wouldn't fail in time."

"Sounds like they made double sure," Red comments.

We're all quiet. Brad studies the grim faces around the table and says, "I have a few more porta-potties. I'll bring them over tomorrow. No extra charge."

Despite the rocky start, the Cowboy Challenge comes off without a hitch. I have to admit it was a great idea and the weekend was fun, even though we were run off our feet. It was almost a holiday atmosphere, with horse people reconnecting with old friends and making new ones. Most came for all three days, and I don't think there were many who missed the final day, when the winner was announced. He went home with a nice pinto PMU rescue gelding in his trailer, that big check in his jeans, and a huge smile on his face.

K.C. and I are in for the night. Mark and Kristy are still putzing around in the Bistro, taking care of little tasks that could just as easily have been put off until the morning. I know why and I think K.C. has figured it out too.

"Hope the septic systems test out okay tomorrow so we can get those trenches buried again," I say. "Bad enough there's going to be the mud. Now there's another bill to deal with."

"Yeah. It takes a bite out of the profit," K.C. agrees.

"At least there was profit to take a bite out of," I say. "Brad's going to give us a deal, but it's still going to mean we'll barely break even. Thank God Kristy and Mark worked for nothing." I say.

"Yeah, they worked their tails off, too. Where are they, anyhow?" K.C. asks.

"Just finishing a few things, then they'll come up."

"Both of them?"

"Well, you know Kristy's staying here, and it won't kill us to have a nightcap with Mark to thank him for all he did."

"If that's all it is," K.C. says, and snorts.

"You forget what it was like being a single guy?"

"No. I just don't like the idea of having to face Jim the next time I see him if Kristy and Mark do the nasty in the bedroom right next to ours." He snorts. "Don't look at me like that. It wouldn't be the first time she boffed a guy within minutes of meeting him."

"Not minutes," I point out. "You make her sound like a floozy."

"Pfft! Hours, then. You call her a free spirit, and you know I like her just fine, but you have to admit she's free with her favors." He has a point. He saw her in action when we lived in Katawasis Lake, after all.

"I'll be sure and let them know it's verboten. Okay?"

"Okay," K.C. says. He takes a long drink of beer, then adds, "This Cowboy Challenge—I think we should make it an annual event. How was the gate?"

"Pretty good," I reply. "I'll show you the dailies."

"Can you pull my boots off first? Please?" he asks. It's not something I usually do, but I feel sorry for him because he looks exhausted, and since he's off the oxy, he's also in pain. I get up, grab a boot, and pull it off. I'm working on the second boot when there's a knock on the door—Stu's customary triple rap—and I hear the door open.

"We're in here," I call out.

"Hey, guys," he says as he comes through the kitchen to join us in the living room.

"Lindy'll get you a beer," K.C. says.

"Naw, after the phone call I just had, I need a scotch."

The boot comes off with a swish. I drop it, look at Stu, and as I'm heading for the liquor cabinet, ask, "What's up?"

"Goddamn Russ," he replies, and goes to flop down in the armchair. If we're exhausted, Stu, being a couple decades older, must be dead on his feet.

"Scotch it is," I tell him, and go to the kitchen, get a glass, and pour in two fingers of Johnny Walker. When I return with the drink and hand it to him, I ask, "What's this about goddamn Russ?"

"The asshole called me."

"Russ called you?"

"Ay-yuh. Soon as the operator asked if I'd accept a collect call from the Kingston Pen, I should have hung up. I was stupid enough to think maybe he wanted our opinion of how good Newt is being took care off."

"And that wasn't it?"

"Nope. Never even asked 'bout the boy. I had a thought to tell him how much we're enjoying our grandson. We seen his first steps. Cute li'l bugger calls me Gampy. You know, I figured to rub salt in the wound. But he just wanted to know did we find out if floating shit attracts rats. Said something like, his offer to buy the place still stands, minus a deduction since it's infested with rats. Then he laughed like a demon and hung up."

I draw a deep breath. "Well, I guess any doubts we might've had about who's behind the sabotage of our septic systems have been laid to rest. But the rat? Wonder how they managed that."

"Will it be enough to change Sergeant Coleman's mind about arresting anyone, though?" Stu wonders.

"No. It might make him believe us, but it's not evidence. There's nothing connecting Trina to it, and Russ always has that ironclad alibi. Just like the murder of Rocky and the vandalism of our irrigation."

"If I'd of recorded it somehow, maybe," Stu says. "You got any kind of spy gadget I could put on our phone so it's ready if he calls again, Lindy?"

"I do, but he's a cagey bugger. He never flat out admitted anything, and he never will, and unless he agreed to let you record the conversation, it's illegal and couldn't be used as evidence. What I want to know is, how do we defend ourselves against another attack? For starters, we can put the barn off limits to anyone except us and our boarders. But we can't stop customers from using the washrooms. Now we know to keep an eye out for a sudden uptick in people with diaper bags, but anyone can have a baggie of bleach concentrate in their jacket pocket. No way of knowing who it could be."

"Maybe we start dumping in that septic tank treatment Brad was talking about," K.C. suggests. "That's easy enough."

"Makes sense," I agree. "But it makes me worry about what their next move will be."

"Tell you what," Stu says, "never thought I'd say it, but the money spent on sprinklers for the Bistro is looking like a damn good thing."

At one a.m. my eyes pop open. What woke me? I'm used to K.C.'s snoring, so that's not it. I listen for sounds outside, but hear nothing. Random thoughts stewing in my brain must be what woke me. Then I realize what, in particular, I didn't think of when Stu told us about Russ' phone call.

I turn on my bedside lamp, and nudge K.C. with my elbow. He stops snoring, but only for a second. I nudge harder. He grumbles and finally growls, "What?"

"I was thinking about Russ phoning Stu."

"Jesus, Lindy, not now." He rolls onto his side, so his back is to me, and pulls the covers up to his ears.

"Yeah, now," I insist. "You know it's two hours later in Ontario?"

"Sure. So that makes it, what? Four? All the lucky people in Ontario are asleep. Just like I was until a minute ago."

"Well, think about it. Stu came to tell us about the phone call right after it happened, am I right?"

"Yeah? So?"

"That was what? Eight thirty? Nine?"

K.C. turns back to face me, and says, "Oh."

"Oh, is right. Isn't that after lockdown? What kind of jam does he have to get to make a phone call at that hour? At least one of the guards must be on the take in order for Russ to get that kind of special treatment."

"Goddammit," K.C. says.

Russ is locked up for life, but we're still not rid of him. A sense of doom settles over me.

# Chapter 12

Sgt. Coleman might not pay attention to my suspicions, but Felix does. He shared one harrowing experience with me, and although he may have blamed me for that, he never said so, and was damn glad I was suspicious enough to turn up when I did. So, when I tell him there's something fishy about Beer Belly Boy, he believes me. Although he can't go with me in an official capacity, and in fact will lose his job if we get caught even though we're going when he's off duty, he agrees to accompany me. He said we just have to make sure we don't get caught.

We haven't told anyone. Red would say she thought Felix had learned his lesson after what happened when he went along with my last hairbrained idea, and K.C. would say he thought I liked Felix more than to rope him into one of my crazy escapades. So, it's better if they don't know.

Ordinarily, I'd be needed in the Bistro because it's Lucy's afternoon off, but first thing in the morning, I whine about having P.I. work and on top of that, there's a report I have to mail and I'm out of stamps. K.C. clicks his tongue and points out these are problems of my own making. Kristy takes the hint and offers to work my shift, saying she's happy to do it because she'd be down there anyway. Mark has been spending a lot of time in the Bistro, so that may have something to do with why she offered so quickly. They've spent every evening together since the Cowboy Challenge. By now they've seen *Dances with Wolves,* the only movie playing in Maple Creek, three times. Kristy says she would happily see it a fourth time, even just to look at Kevin Costner. Can't argue with that.

It would tip my hand if Felix and I left together, so instead of coming to Wacasko-Wâti, he parked in the back lot at Billie's. I pick him up there, and we're off to Swift Current. The first order of business is to drive by Swift Taxi and confirm BBB's truck is there. We see him in the window of the little shed.

"He's picking his nose," I say.

"You're imagining it," Felix says.

"Nope. I'm sure."

"You just don't like him."

"Well, that's true. But it's past his usual quitting time. I wish he'd quit picking his nose and go."

A woman comes into his office. "His replacement," Felix says. He must be right, because he gets up, the woman slides into his chair, and in minutes he's in his truck driving away. We follow him to Dogpatch. I pull off on a side road to wait for him to come back out.

I reach the lunch box out from behind the seat, pull out the mugs and thermos, and pour coffee for both of us. "Two of the sandwiches are roast beef and the rest are chicken. Help yourself."

"Great. Thanks," Felix replies, and digs in. "Hope he doesn't come back before I have a chance to finish these off," he says between mouthfuls.

"Well, one of those is for me, don't forget. And you could save something for the ride home. He usually only stays for about half an hour. You can't possibly eat them all in that time."

"Umm—"

"Never mind trying to prove me wrong."

Two hours later, the sandwiches along with the coffee are long gone before we see his truck heading back out.

"About time," I grouse. I'm starting to be in desperate need of a toilet. "Nearly two hours? In the dark, yet? I've never known him to stay there so long, even in daylight. By now he's missed his dinner."

When I see his taillights disappear over the tracks, I pull out into the street. It hasn't been plowed, and the snow is six or eight inches deep, so it's easy to see no one else has driven here. His tracks turn in to his house as if he parked right at the front stoop, and there are none any farther. The snow is no problem for my truck, so I continue into the pristine snow to the end of the road and around to the back lane and my usual parking spot in the wildly overgrown caragana hedge. I tuck my purse under the seat, grab my flashlight, get out and lock the doors.

"Didn't you say you were going to pick the lock on the front door?" Felix asks as we approach the back of the house.

"Yeah," I reply. "The back door is boarded up. See?"

The beam from his cop-size flashlight plays across the back wall, then focuses on the plywood in the middle. "Easier to pull the plywood off than to fart around picking a lock." The floorboards creek ominously as he climbs up on the verandah to take a closer look.

"I didn't bring a screwdriver," I tell him. "Anyhow, it's faster to pick the lock than undo all those."

"I guess you didn't look very close. They're nails, not screws. I just need to pry the plywood open far enough to get through." He slips his fingers under the edge of the plywood, but can't get enough leverage to tug it open. "I can do it with your tire iron. I'll go get it. Behind the seat, I guess?"

"I'll get it," I say, and head back to the truck. When I have the tool in question, I return to join him on the porch and hand it to him. He pries off one side of the plywood and pulls it out far enough to open the door. We both squeeze inside.

We find ourselves in the surprisingly warm kitchen. I shine my flashlight around, then go to the wood stove on the far side of the small room. "How is it warm in here? If there was a fire in this thing, it went out long before we saw him leave."

"If he lit a fire in it, the whole house would go up or he'd die from the smoke," Felix says, and shines his flashlight on the chimney. There's a large gap where a section of the pipe has fallen away.

"So, how is there heat with no power?"

"Good question."

"I suppose there's no chance there's a toilet in this place," I mutter.

There's no furniture other than the battered kitchen table buried by the stack of beer, and surprisingly, wine boxes.

"Look at that! There's as many wine boxes as beer cartons. I wouldn't've taken him for a wine drinker," I say.

"Could drink both," Felix says. "Lucky's the cheapest beer going and nothing that comes in a box is wine snob wine."

"I guess not," I agree. "No signs of renovations. If he's fixing anything, it's not the kitchen."

"I guess he hadn't got far when he got hurt."

"He was never hurt. Or at least not so badly he couldn't do anything. He has no plans to renovate this shack, he just has it for some other reason. He's hiding something, and if not a victim, something else illegal. That's why we're here."

"Well, I know you think that, but maybe you're not right this time, Auntie," Felix says, and leads the way into the front room.

A couple of doors open off it, but as in the kitchen, there's no evidence of any repairs, and not surprisingly, neither room is a bathroom. After five minutes, I draw a deep breath and say, "Well, this is a bust. Surely, he doesn't come here just to get away from his wife."

"You never know how far someone will go to get away from their wife." He shines his flashlight on my face and adds, "Or husband."

I get his meaning, but refuse to take the bait, turn away, and say, "Let's get out of here. How about a steak at The Pioneer House? My treat."

"Perfect," he says, and we head back outside.

While Felix taps the nails to put the plywood back in place, he says, "He's going to know someone was messing with this. Can't get all the nails back in very good. Tire iron ain't meant for pounding nails."

"Besides that, there's all the tracks," I tell him, and shine the beam of my flashlight on the footsteps in the snow.

"Maybe that blizzard we're supposed to get in the next couple days will cover them."

"Doubt it matters. He'll think it was the drag racers I told you about. No way of tracing any of this to us."

"Hope you're right."

I hope so, too.

Dinner is great. We have plenty of Rocking R business to discuss, so the talk isn't all me reiterating why I've got such an obsession with BBB or bitching about the bikers and their parties. Felix has complaints of his own. He has humorous anecdotes about his RCMP experiences, but claims the Department is a toxic work environment, and he lays the blame for that squarely at Sgt. Coleman's feet.

"I'm starting to understand why you call him Rosco," he says. "You know, I told Gerard about that.

"Oh, no! You didn't!"

"I did. Don't worry, we all call him that now. Behind his back, of course."

"Of course. Just don't let it slip."

"Well, if I do, I'll just have to tell him where I got it from. Think about that, the next time you try to rope me into cleaning stalls."

We're out of bread and eggs. "I'll make porridge," I offer.

K.C. snorts and frowns. "How many times have you been in town this week, and you couldn't get groceries?"

"I'll go today. But anyway, what's wrong with porridge?"

"I don't want porridge."

I nearly tell him he sounds like a petulant child, but instead, I say, "I'll go to the Bistro and borrow some bread and eggs, then."

"Why don't I just go eat breakfast there?" he suggests.

Fact is, I think that's a good solution, other than I wonder why he didn't say *we* instead of *I*. I make a mental note to schedule a serious talk about his mental health.

There's new snow covering our pathway to the Bistro. I hope Swift Current got as much as we did so all our tracks are covered. I barely hear K.C.'s grumbling until he says he's going to buy a snowblower. "Not this year, please. It's what? Ten feet from the porch to where Stu plowed with the tractor? Easy enough to shovel that," I say.

"Why don't you do it, then."

Maybe it's our marriage and not his mental health that needs examining. I stop to give Henry some ear scratches and let K.C. get a good distance ahead of me before the mental image of me kicking him in the ass becomes more than fantasy. By the time I enter the Bistro, he's already sitting at the staff table. I go into the kitchen to let Barney know what I want. When I return, Kristy, who had been circulating with the carafe, topping up everyone's coffee and chatting with all the customers, is at our table, filling a couple of mugs.

"Thanks, Kristy," I say.

Just then, the cowbell over the door clangs. I look up to see Mark coming in, with Felix right behind him. Mark being here isn't unusual, but Felix, at this hour, is.

As he approaches Kristy, Mark loops an arm around her, gives her a quick kiss, and says, "Good morning, hon."

"Quit it! I'm working," she scolds. "Sit, and I'll join you in a sec. You want menus?"

"I already know what I want," Mark says, and utters a low growl as he gives her a parting squeeze.

I glance at K.C. His black expression makes obvious what he thinks of that. I give him a kick under the table. He rewards me with a scowl equally as intense as the one he just gave Mark and Kristy.

"Can't stick around," Felix replies, and sets a thermos on the table. "Could I just get you to fill this? And I'd like a couple rat turds to go," Felix says. "Maybe make it four. And stick a cinnamon bun in there." He slides into the chair beside me to wait.

"I don't need a menu either," Mark says. He releases Kristy and takes the chair across from me. "I'll have the Winemaker's Breakfast."

"Sure thing," Kristy says.

As she scoots off, I ask Felix, "Why the big rush? Thought you were trimming bulls' hooves today."

"That was the plan, but I've been called in."

"Oh yeah? Accident somewhere?" I ask.

"Not exactly," he replies, and looks around the room before continuing in a low voice. "A body's been found. Don't say nothing, but looks like it's that woman that went missing from around here a while back."

I draw a deep breath as my guts clench.

"They've got you investigating?" K.C. asks.

"No, I ain't that important," he says, and sighs. "I'm relieving the conservation guys. That's who found her. Apparently, they were patrolling for poachers, followed tracks leading down a road no one with good intentions would be using, when they seen what looked like a vehicle had went off the road and got stuck. Seen something half buried in snow, figured it was a deer, turned out to be a body, not a deer. I'll secure the site until Major Crimes shows up. Keep everyone away, like there's going to be traffic. But you never know. If some reporter's been listening to a police scanner, it could get busy."

"Where?" I ask. "I mean, where was she found?"

"South of town. Looks like he was heading for the back way into the Badlands. Almost made it, too. Half a mile or so from where the road ends, they said. Stupid to try and go there in whiteout conditions."

"Stupid, maybe, but good thing he did."

"That's right," he replies, "or she might not of been found until spring, especially with another blizzard coming. That road's so bad, you can barely call it a road at the best of times. I'm taking the Bronco from the motor pool." He shrugs and adds, "Gonna be cold and boring. Another shit assignment."

"Everyone has to pay their dues," K.C. says.

"Yeah, I know," Felix agrees.

"You know, driving around in bad conditions like that," I begin, "have you guys thought about how much work it is to be a murderer?"

"No, Lindy," K.C. says, "no one but you thinks about stuff like that."

"Think about it, though. The guy—and I say *guy* because serial killers are usually men—has to be big enough to pack a body around. Even a small human is going to be a hundred pounds. Think of a hundred-pound feed sack. Fifty pounds is bad enough. But say he's really strong. He also has to have driving skills and a truck, probably a four by four, to make it that far on that road. And then when he's almost there, he gets stuck and has to dig his vehicle out. More hard work! But he gets it done and still has to offload the body. He can't leave it on the road because it might be discovered before he has a chance to get out of the area, so he humps it a ways off and throws some snow over it. Not ideal, but what choice does he have? He has to be gone before anyone comes along. Damn!"

"Impressed, are you?"

"Well, maybe a little, not in a good way, of course. It does paint a picture of the murderer. It's what profilers do."

"So, now you're a profiler? And your profile is that he's a strong guy who has a four-wheel drive truck and can drive in snow, like every other rancher in this part of the country. Jesus, Lindy," K.C. says.

"What if he has a helper?" Kristy asks. She's just come from the kitchen with Felix's take out in time to hear the last bit of our conversation. She hands Felix his order and adds, "He wouldn't have to be big. It could be two skinny runts."

"Kristy, you're right!" I exclaim. "I never thought of that! So maybe even a couple. Women can be big and strong, too, but even if she wasn't, she would still be able to help—"

"Just listen to the two of you," K.C. says. "No way a woman is going to go along with that."

"You wouldn't think so, but they do," I correct him. "It's rare but not unheard of, and it's even been in the news lately. That guy in California who called himself the Folsom Wolf. He and his girlfriend just got the death penalty. First time since California reinstated capital punishment and, I think, the first time for a woman—"

K.C. waves dismissively, turns to Mark and says, "Mark, since the hoof trimming is off, any chance you could help Stu with the vats?"

"I think so," Mark replies.

"Good. That'll free me up," K.C. says. "Come out to the vats when you're finished eating." He gets up and walks off.

Free him up? What does he have to be freed up for? There were no lessons on the board last I checked. But as I watch his back disappearing out the door, my thoughts turn to Kristy's suggestion that a woman could be involved. It would explain why Janey might take a ride with strangers. Likewise for the young woman whose body was just found. And she was dumped on the back way into the Badlands. The road is off the grid, not really a road but an easement, barely maintained, and not many people even know about it. Exactly the same way the killer or killers got into the Badlands to dump Lucy's body. Coincidence? I don't think so.

"Lindy?" Mark says, interrupting my thoughts.

I reply, "Yes?"

"I haven't had a chance to talk to you alone, Lindy. About the Cowboy Challenge."

"What about it?"

"Well, I was wondering. Is Clay Ridley a friend?"

"Who?"

"Clay Ridley."

"Never heard of him."

"Oh." He shovels an impressive blob of scrambled egg, cheese, mushroom, and bacon into his mouth, then chews and swallows before continuing "So, you didn't recognize him in the crowd. Could he be a friend of K.C.'s?"

"I don't think so. What's going on?"

"Well, I saw K.C. talking to him."

"I'm sure he talked to a lot of people."

"Yeah. But Clay is a dealer, Lindy."

"What? Like a, er, pusher? Like, a heroin pusher?"

"Pharmaceuticals mainly. He's a friend of Trina's, that's how I know. You don't want him hanging around here."

"No, I sure don't! But I don't know what he looks like, so how—"

"If I see him when I'm here sometime, I'll point him out. But more likely he won't come unless you put on another big event like Cowboy Challenge. Then you'll need someone on the gate to make sure guys like him don't get in. I volunteer," he says, "and I work for beer."

We share a chuckle, but it's really not funny.

K.C. was circulating the entire weekend, so it's not surprising he would have talked to that Clay guy. Surely that's all there is to it. But a guy pushing pharmaceuticals such as Oxy, maybe? With no prescription for oxycodone, is K.C. getting them elsewhere? Now I've got something else to worry about.

# Chapter 13

Historically, Wacasko-Wâti Christmas decorations go up soon after we take down the Halloween ones, and that's the topic of discussion around the staff table this morning. The Christmas tree farm dropped off our two twelve-footers yesterday. The boxes of decorations were hauled down from the hayloft earlier. Tomorrow being Monday, the Bistro is closed, but we'll have the usual staff come in anyway, and they can take care of it. We'll do the draw of names for the staff Secret Santa tomorrow, too.

"Don't put my name in the Secret Santa draw," Felix says.

"What's that? Did I hear a *bah, humbug*?" I ask.

"No, that ain't it. It's just that I ain't going to be here."

"Where else would you be?" Red demands.

"You know I didn't qualify for the Finals. I'm fixing that, starting with rodeos this winter." Even before the Cowboy Challenge, Felix was grumbling about not qualifying for the National Finals Rodeo. His is trip to Edmonton to take in some of the events this year got him more worked up about it than before.

"What did you expect? You never rode in but a few rodeos," Red points out. "You could go to more, starting in the spring."

"I know, Auntie," Felix says. He sighs and drains his mug. "This past season I figured it was more important to concentrate on my business. And at first it was cool to be an auxiliary, but it pays nothing and takes me away from my real work. Taught me something, though."

"Oh yeah? What?" I ask.

"Same problem I had back in school. Getting ordered around? Not for me. I ain't cut out to be any sort of military guy. Might've been okay if Dwight was still the big cheese, but—don't tell no one I said this—that little pipsqueak is on my ass all the time and it's getting on my wick. Sits on his skinny keister and orders everyone around."

"Rank has its privilege," K.C. says. "Can't be too useless or he wouldn't be where he is."

"You ever heard the expression, it ain't what you know, it's who you blow? I think that's how he got where he is," Felix says. "No matter. I'll be finished with what I signed up for pretty quick. Already put in my notice. I'm out of there. Besides, I ain't getting any younger. If I want a championship, I'm going to have to get after it."

"You've got time," I tell him. "There's always next year."

"Yeah. Always next year and I'm already pushing thirty. Meanwhile, I'm stuck here with nothing to do all winter but fill the feeders and make sure the trough heaters are working. Anyone can do that."

"Russ used to take stock down to rodeos all over the States, winter *and* summer," Red says. "Why not sign up for that course to get your Class 1 licence? Then you can deliver stock to the rodeos and ride in them too."

"Yeah, you know that's tough to pull off. I believe Russ quit riding when he got busy with the stock. Anyhow, it's too late for this winter and right now I got bucking stock lounging around eating me out of house and home. Exactly the reason you were looking to sell in the first place. You warned me before we made our deal. Dunno why I thought I could do anything different.

The semen business is good, steady, and we got enough frozen to fill any orders we get between now and spring. The money I make from the ranch is okay, but I can make more winning a few events down south doing something I love. So that's where I'm heading."

"What? You're heading south?" Stu demands. "Who's going to look after things here?"

"You know Mark quit Trina, right? I put him in charge."

"First I heard of it," I say.

"But Mark ain't... I mean, what does he know about looking after the stock?" Red asks. "What'll he do if something goes wrong? If one of them gets hurt or sick?"

"He's been helping out since he showed up here, and he's doing good. He can phone the vet as easy as the next guy, plus he can call on Stu or K.C. any time, right?"

"Of course," K.C. says.

"You know it," Stu confirms. "But it ain't the same as having someone on site."

"I was living in the lab, so he'll just slide in there. If I can shower in the wash rack, so can he." With that, he gets to his feet and says, "Don't worry, I ain't leaving right away. I'll swing in here and say goodbye before I go." He gives a little wave and says, "See you, folks."

We watch him go out the door. "Well, I'll be go to hell," Red says. "Wish that kid would just quit the rodeo before he gets hurt."

"Don't look at me like that," Stu says. "I quit."

"Yeah, but not until you were forty something and had how many concussions? I call that getting hurt."

"A few little knocks on the ol' bean never kilt no one."

Red blows out a sharp breath, then says, "Men!"

When she, Stu, and K.C. finish their coffee and leave, too, I stay put, and when I see Kristy coming my way with an empty carafe, I say, "Leave that for now, Kristy. Sit down and join me."

"Sure," she says, "just give me a minute to dispose of this." She indicates the empty carafe by giving it a jiggle and disappears into the kitchen. In a moment, she's sliding onto the chair across from me and sets her mug on the table.

"So, I hear Mark's going to be around permanently, or at least through the winter," I say. "You knew, didn't you, Kristy?"

"I did," she confirms. "I promised not to tell anyone until Felix told you."

"None of my business, maybe, but I'm wondering what it means for you and, um... Or really, um..."

"I know what you're getting at, Lindy, and I wanted to talk to you anyway. About me staying a while longer."

"Kris, you can stay as long as you want to, you know that."

"Good," she exclaims, and exhales loudly. "I figured it would be okay, because, you know, I stayed quite a while last time. Will K.C. be okay with it?"

"My house, my rules." I reply.

At the harsh tone of my voice, she frowns. "What's going on? You and him have always been such a team. In Katawasis Lake, he helped you break into that storage locker. And speaking of Katawasis Lake, all the girls at the barn were after him and he picked you. You were happy about it. So what's wrong now?"

"Nothing," I say. "Well, nothing and everything. Right now, I have to get back to work. And I want you to know it's always great having you here. Although you and I seem to have a knack for getting into trouble."

"Yeah! Good trouble! We're the Katawasis Girls! I've been so frickin' bored with my life in Calgary. All I do is get up, go to work, go home, go to bed, repeat. I've spent *soooo* much time thinking about our adventures. 'Member when I lured Butch into your house so he wouldn't catch us breaking into his, um, where he kept his stuff? Time to dig out my Swiss Army knife and get on with the next case!" She giggles.

"You still have it?"

"Of course. What would I do with it, throw it away? It's small so it doesn't take up any space. Besides, it reminds me of us. Me, you, and Deena, the Katawasis Girls, Detectives at Large. Remember? Instead of pins like the Rotary club, we had matching knives."

"Just the two of us now."

"It's all right. Deena wasn't as into it as me and you. I haven't put it in my bra like we did back then, but I got a nice silver chain for it and sometimes I wear it when I go to work. The rich old fuddy-duddies at The Ranchmen's Club find it amusing. Of course, they don't see it unless I bend over and give them a good look down my shirt."

"You do that often, if I know you."

"You betcha! And then they have to pretend like they weren't looking, but they're dying to know what it is and just *have* to ask. I tease them by slowly pulling it partway out and then claiming it's stuck. Let them fantasize about getting it out for me. I get the best tips of anyone."

"No surprise. Just remember you have it if you have to go through a metal detector." We both stand and she gives me a hug before heading into the kitchen.

I hope she never regrets being so eager for adventure.

⁂

Monday, Kristy and I are in my truck, destination feed store because we're nearly out of crushed oats and sweet feed, the tack shop because Kristy wants western shirts, and Millie's Ladies

Wear because we both want something pretty for Christmas. Kristy is definitely here for an extended period.

Forty-five minutes with just the two of us in the truck is a good chance for a real, private, heart-to-heart. This time, her reason for wanting a reprieve from her marriage is more than boredom. Now Jim's ex plays a bigger part.

"He never sticks up for me, Lindy," Kristy says. "You should hear his side of the conversation. Yes, dear. No dear. Can I kiss your ass, dear? He's quit telling me what she's accused me of, but I know it's more of the same: something horrible I did to one of the brats, such as telling them to pick up after themselves. And on top of it all, he pays increased child support because the kids are bigger and need more expensive stuff now. As if they had to have the latest video game and it couldn't wait until Christmas. And she needs more alimony because, you know, inflation. You'd think Pissy could have the decency to marry her asshole boyfriend so the alimony would stop, wouldn't you?"

"Um, I guess she thinks it makes sense. Why give up that extra income? K.C.'s ex hasn't remarried either. The alimony is a big expense for him, too. It sure would be nice to put those dollars into our joint account."

"Exactly what I mean. Anyhow, I've about had it."

Just then, something else seizes my attention: a familiar truck parked at Billie's. It's not like there's anything unique about BBB's truck, and he should be at work a hundred miles away, so it's likely not his. There is, however, one white motorcycle with a war bonnet headlight. We're past the entrance before I noticed it, or I would've driven into the lot to confirm that's really what I saw. Should I find a place to turn around and go back?

"Are you even listening to me?" Kristy asks, breaking into my thoughts.

I glance at her and say, "I, er, sorry, Kris. I missed that last part."

"So, you can't drive and listen at the same time?"

"Busy mind," I say. The truck likely isn't BBBs, and anyone could have bought the Indian from the dealer where Mark traded it. I abandon the idea of turning back. "What were you saying?"

"Never mind. Just more of the same. What about you and K.C.?"

"Also more of the same. I told you he's been making a lot of long-distance phone calls to an unlisted number? Like a few times a week? He even lied when I asked him who he called. Said he didn't call anyone, but since then, the calls to the unlisted number have stopped. He should realize that I'm like the Gestapo. I haff vays."

"So, who do you think he's calling?"

"His ex, I think. If not her, then maybe a girlfriend."

"Sounds like phone fucks to me," Kristy says, and gives me a sideways look.

I'm used to her using the F-word and everyone's using it more these days, so I don't react. "Yeah. That's what I think, too."

"What are you going to do about it?"

"You know me. I have a plan."

One dog is a dog, but two dogs is a pack, and a pack does things one dog on its own would never even think of. Kristy and I are a pack.

On Thursday, I tell everyone I have Christmas shopping to do. Kristy and I head out mid-morning. I aim the van around the back of Billie's, park just past the corner of the building to command a view of the road and turn the engine off. "Now all we have to do is be sure we don't get distracted and miss him when he goes by," I say.

"How long do you think we'll have to wait?" Kristy asks.

"Dunno. You said last time he left within minutes of me leaving the yard. So maybe not long."

"I just wonder if we'll be able to be able to follow him on these open roads without being made. If we stay far enough back that he can't see us, he can turn off anywhere without us seeing him, too."

"True," I agree. "But if he does see us, don't worry. He won't confront me, because if he does, he'll have to come up with an excuse for going to town. He usually just tells me what to get for him. Then I ask him about all the phone calls, and suddenly that changes? Give me a break."

"He could say he's doing some Christmas shopping, same as us," Kristy says. She digs through her purse for the compact that's seldom far from her hand.

"You need to fix your makeup already?"

"I left the Bistro without fixing it," she tells me.

"Oh. It's important, then. So much could have happened since then." Of course, I'm teasing. She's used to that and doesn't stop, just gives me a sideways look and returns her attention to her task.

"So. Do you think a Billie's Pub T-shirt would look good on me?"

"Um, what?" She snaps the compact shut and drops it in her purse, then looks at me and says, "Well, sure, I guess. Kind of a dumb idea, though."

"Yup, a dumb idea, wearing advertising for a competitor. But if he's not coming here to buy me a shirt, what other reason could he have?" I point at K.C.'s truck as it turns into the parking lot.

"That's weird," Kristy says.

"Wonder how long he's going to stay."

"I hope not long, because I really do want to shop."

But K.C.'s visit to Billie's doesn't cut into our shopping time. His truck is out on the road, heading back to Wacasko-Wâti in under ten minutes. Long enough to have a beer? I guess so, but I can't figure out why he would go there to chugalug a beer when we have our own. He must have gone to meet someone, but again, for ten minutes? Maybe he really did just go in to buy a shirt.

At least it leaves us plenty of time to shop.

When we're shopped out and the stores are closing, we treat ourselves to dinner at The Jasper, so it's late by the time we're home. We see Wacasko-Wâti long before we come to it, thanks to Christmas lights all around the Bistro building, and on the pillars and posts of the patio. Everything looks festive and cheery. The Bistro itself is dark, but the lights in the barn and arena are on.

"K.C. must be still teaching," I say. "Didn't know he had lessons this late."

Kristy and I are barely in the house with our purchases when there's a quick tap on the door and Red bursts in. This can't be good.

"How come you gals're so late getting home?" Red demands.

"Well, we—"

"Never mind," she says. "Remember that box of chicken on the floor when we had that flood? And the rat?"

"Well, yeah, but the chicken on the floor was an isolated incident. Same with the rat. Not a serious rat invasion or anything. No big deal."

"Well, it wouldn't be a big deal, if not for the Health Inspection Agency finding out. So, them bastards shut us down."

"*What?*"

"Yeah. We got to have a partner meeting."

In the morning, with the *Sorry – Closed* notice on the door, other than going out to explain to a couple of regulars that showed up that we had to shut down because a pipe burst, we have nothing to do other than sit around the staff table, swilling multiple pots of coffee and eating day-old pastry. The kitchen's closed. No need for that today, so no staff. No worry about privacy.

Red lays the papers the inspector left with her on the table, and says, "We're shut down because of one damn rat and a box on the floor."

I glance at the citation, then focus on the photo. "No question this is our rat, on our floor," I conclude.

"Yeah, for sure," Red agrees. "Me and Stu figured whoever done it made like to go to the bathroom, then came down the back hall. Wouldn't of had to of come right into the kitchen, could just stick the rat around the corner when no one was looking. So, it was someone who knew they could get to the kitchen that way."

"Trina, I'm betting. She planned to sneak in when everyone was distracted with the flood," I reply. "The adjoining hall just made it easy for her."

"We're going to have to put a door just past the washrooms. And keep it locked."

"That's a good idea, Red. And I'll get the inspector on the phone and see if we can't get him to come back for a chat. Maybe just give us a warning this time. But these are just knee-jerk reactions, nothing pro-active. Time to do something to put them out of business permanently. We need to cut the head off the snake."

"How do we do that?" Red asks.

"I have no idea."

In fact, no one has any idea how to we might put Trina and her crew out of business, mostly because they don't seem to have any business other than charging a fee for anyone to party, camp or bunk there. "Not much though. Kind of like a hostel," Mark explains. "No other source of income I could see."

"They shipped the last of their cattle, so no more ranch income, although the sale of that one good bucking bull would be enough to keep her afloat for quite a while. I can't even give you guys a raise to increase her expenses," I say, and lean back with a sigh. "All she'll owe is forty percent of the property tax and mortgage payments. And how much Benson has socked away is a complete unknown, so we don't know what it would take to drive her into bankruptcy."

"Well, they still have to eat, pay the electric and gas, so they gotta be getting money from somewhere," Red says.

"I'm sure Russ supports them," I say. "If only we could find out where he stashed his money and how he's laundering it. I thought it would be through the ranch, but since they didn't buy more cattle, that can't be it. Mark, in your job you must've seen some pretty creative bookkeeping."

"I'm not in the fraud section. But the membership or user fees, whatever you want to call them?" Mark says. "She could be inflating those. All she'd have to do is up the number of guests.

Nice little cash business, and a tax auditor would expect her to be claiming less, rather than more. I bet if we could get a look at her books, we'd find her claimed income from fees and renting bunks is a helluva lot more than would jive with the traffic we see coming and going."

"Great idea," I say. "How can we do that, get a look at her books?"

"Hey, I can tell you the what," Mark says. "Up to you to figure out the how."

No one can do anything other than mumble. "Come on, people!" I say. "With all the brain power, higher education and life experience here, surely someone can come up with something."

When there's still nothing but mumbling, Kristy says, "Guys, I don't mean to horn in, but I have an idea."

When we gathered for this meeting, we invited her to sit with us, but she declined, saying it wasn't her business, but she hovered around the coffee bar and pastry case, giving everything a surplus cleaning. She was so much in the background I had almost forgotten she was there. Now we all turn to face her.

"Sorry," she says.

"Don't be," I say. "There are no bad ideas. Come and sit down and tell us what you're thinking."

# Chapter 14

We're back in business! At least temporarily, pending an inspection, which will happen with no advance warning in the not-too-distant future. Everyone loves a surprise, right?

When I give everyone the news, I say, "I think the last so-called inspector planted the rat. Why else didn't he tell us he was here?"

"Why would he do that?" K.C. asks.

"Because Russ got to him."

"That's ridiculous," K.C. opines. "Russ doesn't have that kind of reach."

"Russ *does* have that kind of reach. You know any other maximum security inmates who can make phone calls after lights out? If you think that Russ couldn't get to a provincial food inspector, you're the one that's ridiculous." That was out of my mouth before I remembered that Christmas is coming up and I should be nicer if I don't want coal in my stocking. Come to think of it, coal might be preferable to a Billie's T-shirt.

The last time we were shut down, the Food Inspection Agency didn't even have a record of it. The notice was counterfeit. The big money guys orchestrated it. Why? They wanted our land because they had advance knowledge that our road was going to be upgraded to connect the Trans Canada Highway to Cypress Hills Interprovincial Park and Fort Walsh historical site, making it a prime commercial development opportunity. They were right. Since then, our road is busier than ever, and it accounts for much of the success of our business. It was before K.C.'s time, but they got to an inspector, one that actually showed up, so why couldn't Russ/Trina do the same? K.C. didn't respond. Or at least I didn't hear him if he did, because I went outside and closed the door behind me.

The new door closing off the hall to the washroom is drywalled, primed and painted. While we were at it, we gave the whole kitchen a fresh coat of paint and we've scrubbed, scoured and disinfected until you could perform surgery here. The inspector should be impressed.

This morning, I've come down to pick up the Johnson's Supply invoices, and Kristy confronts me as I'm leaving.

"So, you're leaving without talking to me? Really? I'm *so* done with this place!" she declares. Really a lot louder than she has to, and in the middle of the Bistro instead of at the house, or at least back in the kitchen.

"What's wrong?"

"You know what's wrong!'

"Let's talk about it, but not here. Come up to my office." There's a sickening, whiny tone in my voice. "Please?"

"I'll come up all right, but just long enough to get my things."

"But Kristy—"

"No *but Kristy!* I'm done talking. Some friend you turned out to be. All the work I do around here, and now you increase the rent right after you lay me off, as if you weren't charging enough on that one little room!"

"It's not personal, Kris, just business."

"Well, I'm *done* with your business!" She storms out the door, leaving me standing next to the coffee bar, my face turning red as I shuffle my feet. She had to choose this time, when the seniors that meet for coffee and a chinwag every morning are at the table next to the coffee bar? She was so loud she even got the attention of the guys that are nearly deaf, and now they're all looking at me as if I've just drowned a bag full of puppies.

It's true we don't need her in the Bistro, but Kristy is very popular with old people, even the ladies, even though she wears tight, low-cut T-shirts and short skirts, and bends over often, offering both a view from front and back. It goes without saying she's popular with the men. But it's the nice old ladies who are giving me the evil eye right now. They would be on her side no matter what her complaint was. I guess I shouldn't be surprised that they look so disapproving. I've often seen the same expression on my mother's face.

"Sorry, folks," I tell them. "You know we're heading into our slow season, so..." I sigh, lift my hands in an expression of defeat, turn and hurry out the door and up to my house.

Kristy is in the kitchen making a fresh pot of coffee. When she turns to face me, we both dissolve into uncontrolled laughter. Once our laughter dies down, Kristy wipes the tears from her face and asks, "You think they bought it?"

"Absolutely, they bought it. It'll be all over Maple Creek and surrounding area by tonight," I reply. "I just hope they don't decide I'm so deplorable that they don't want to come here anymore."

"Where else would they go? We're, er, *you're* the closest, other than Billie's, and they're finished their coffee klatch before Billie's even opens. Plus Billie's doesn't have cinnamon buns."

When the coffee's ready we fill our mugs and perch on stools at the island. I ask, "So, is everything ready for you to move?"

"Yup. I'll be leaving for Mark's as soon as I get my car loaded up. And since there's a biker Christmas party coming up, I'll be meeting all those bad boys and telling my sad story. Especially the bit about having to shower in the wash stall."

"You'd better be careful, or you may have an audience."

"Ha! Wouldn't that be fun! Give those guys a cheap thrill. Wonder if that cute blond guy that used to come to help with Butch's business is in Trina's gang."

"Don't be crazy, Kristy. You don't know them. Things could get rough. Don't forget, there's a serial killer at large."

"I know, Lindy."

"I hope you mean that."

"I do. Anyhow, I know you think I'm a Picky Eunice, but it won't really be so bad now that there's shower curtains up around it and they rigged a heater up above it. But anyhow, if Trina doesn't suggest I use the shower at her place, I'll ask her if I can. But not right away. I'll have to hold my nose and suck up to her. You know we didn't get along before."

"I remember. But do you really have to look for work? It seems like a waste of time since I want you back here in the spring."

"Well, I have to, though. Wouldn't be logical for me to hang around waiting to get back on at the Bistro after our blow-up."

"I guess not," I agree. "I'm sure going to miss you, though."

"I know. I'll miss you, too. At least K.C. will be happy. Me being with Mark pisses him off, and now he won't have to see us together. I still don't get it. I never thought he was all that buddy-buddy with Jim."

"I guess he feels a little disloyal. I thought he would chill out once you told Jim you wanted a divorce, you know, so you weren't just sneaking around. Now he'll have to find some other reason to be grouchy. I told you I've been counting his pills, and they seem right, but honestly, I still think he must be flushing them down the toilet."

Kristy slowly shakes her head and says, "He sure has changed. Why, I wonder?"

"Wish I knew. It can't all be because of the medication," I say. "Thinking back on the first couple years we were together, he spent a lot of time away doing clinics. He might have seemed a little off at times, but I didn't think anything of it. He ran interference for me the night I broke into Hal's storage locker and found Jerry's car, and he went with me to Russ' house. In fact, he's the one who found the hidden trophy closet. And now he acts like I'm an idiot for being suspicious of Asselstine. You know the old cliché: familiarity breeds contempt. Everyone's on their best behaviour at first."

"Men!" Kristy says. "Speaking of Assel whozit—do you still think he's the killer? Even after you didn't find nothing at that old shack of his?"

"Yeah, it's still rattling around in the back of my mind. I can't stop wondering how it could be warm even though there was no source of heat. Or why he was in Maple Creek when he should've been at work a hundred miles away. The first time I saw him in town, Janey's body was found in the Badlands the next day. Coincidence? Cops and P.I.s don't believe in coincidences."

"So, you're thinking maybe there's something in the old house that he needs to keep warm."

"Right. But we didn't find anything that could be damaged by freezing. The woodstove couldn't have been used because the chimney wasn't connected, and there was no other heater."

"What if there's a hidden space, like Russ' trophy storage closet, and he's got a little heater in there."

"That's what bothers me. But what kind of little heater?"

"Um, well, not electric, I guess," Kristy says, and sighs. "So, maybe there's a woodstove in the basement."

"It would need a chimney. And there's no basement."

"Maybe me and you ought to go check it out again."

"You know, I've been wanting to go back. But we can't be seen together. So, when we need a Katawasis Girl meeting place, we can use Jesse's lunchroom. We'll set up a time that I can be away for a day. I'll call and meet you there."

"Jesse's okay with that?"

"Yup. He thinks my cloak and dagger stuff is hilarious."

"It kinda is."

"Park in the alley. There's a back door."

The seniors have continued to come for their morning conflab, so I guess I'm forgiven. Maybe it helped that we laid off all the staff except Marcie, Lily and Barney, so they believed I was telling the truth when I said it was a business decision.

K.C. might be glad Kristy isn't staying with us anymore, but I miss her. I'm looking forward to our meeting at Jesse's today. I park on the street as usual and go inside. Jesse has someone with him in his office, so I chat with Eileen for a couple minutes before I head back to the lunchroom. I haven't finished my first cup of coffee when there's a knock at the door. I let Kristy in.

She greets me with: "Good news, Lindy! I've got a job."

"Already?"

"Yup. Did you know Billie's is hiring?"

"Billie's? How do they need to hire when I've had to lay people off?"

"Completely different clientele, Lindy. I seen them when I went in to apply for the job. They're a rougher bunch. Plus they got stuff, entertaining stuff like pool tables, TVs everywhere, a dance floor, a juke box plus live music on weekends, and buck a beer at happy hour. I guess that's their busy time, because I'm booked for nothing so far but four hour shifts covering happy hour."

I'm so pissed at Billie's having a better business plan than ours, wondering whether we could compete by starting our own happy hour, pushing some tables together to make room for dancing, and putting in a joke box, that I'm speechless.

"You must of known they had bands on the weekends," Kristy continues.

"I guess I did. I just didn't think it was something we could, or should, do. K.C.'s been harping about getting a four-tap Kegerator so we could offer more brands of draft. Maybe it's not such a bad idea."

"You don't want the Billie's crowd. Believe me." She fills a mug of hours-old coffee, and slides onto the chair across from me. "Are we going to go to BBB's pretty quick? Because I start at Billie's on Wednesday."

"How about tomorrow?"

<hr>

"What excuse did you give Mark for coming with me tonight?" I ask.

"Christmas shopping. In Swift Current. Same one you gave K.C."

"Good thing the stores are open late for Christmas shopping now. But we're still going to be late getting home. We'll have to say we saw a movie or went for drinks or maybe dinner at The Pioneer House. He made some comment about me doing a lot of Christmas shopping lately and asked where I have the gifts stashed. I just said *wouldn't you like to know*, all coy like, you know? So, it's a good thing we're stopping at the tack shop."

"What are you going to get him?"

"Damned if I know. Probably another shirt, same as always."

"That's as good as anything. I should get one for Mark, too."

It's late, of course, because we can't take a chance on BBB being there, so we shop until the store closes at nine, then head for Dogpatch. I have a sleeping bag, a duffle bag containing a few articles of clothing on top, and underneath, a hammer, flashlight, camcorder, and my gun. Kristy has a couple of plastic bags for her kit. Why? Because as unlikely as it is that we'll get caught breaking into BBB's shack, we need a cover story.

Once over the railroad tracks, instead of driving straight ahead, I turn left and park the truck a couple of blocks from the house. The good thing about the snow is that it reflects the moonlight, so although there are no streetlights out here in Dogpatch, the moon is up so it's not too dark. We get to the back porch, and I have no trouble prying the plywood covering the back door open wide enough to let us in. It's all gone well.

Except it's not warm inside. In fact, it's as cold as you'd expect an uninsulated, unoccupied house to be.

"Well, nothing's changed," I say as I shine the flashlight around.

"Other than it's cold," Kristy observes.

"Yeah. Also, I shouldn't say nothing's changed. He's cleared the stacks of wine and beer boxes off the table, and it's in the middle of the room instead of in the corner." I blow out a long breath, defeated. "What a waste of time."

"Maybe not. If it means you'll quit obsessing over this guy, it's not a waste."

"You're right. But I don't think it'll do that."

Kristy hops up to sit on the table, swings her legs, and says, "Oh no? Why not?"

"Well, you know there's no one missing now."

"So, you think this is where he stashes them?"

"Yes, and that's why the house was heated. You know Dwight said he had Janey for two months before he killed her. He had to keep her somewhere that no one could hear her. She could scream her head off here and it wouldn't matter."

"But that was summer, so he wouldn't need heat."

"True. But the woman he grabbed in Maple Creek—that wasn't long ago and I'm betting it's the reason this place was warm when Felix and I came. Remember I told you how long we had to wait for him to leave? He never stayed that long while I was surveilling him. I think that was when he strangled her and dragged her out to his truck. Then he cleared away any evidence of her being in here."

"Still. What did he use for heat, being as he can't light a fire in the stove or plug in a heater?"

"I think he has a kerosene heater. The empty cans in the garage puzzled me for quite a while before I figured that out." If I sound smug, it's because I'm pretty proud of connecting those dots.

Kristy isn't as impressed as I thought she'd be. "But there were no signs of anyone being locked up here? No chains or food wrappers or mattress or anything? Did he haul all that stuff out to the shed and clean up right away as soon as he took her body out, even though he could come back and do it any time?"

"I know. You're right, it's a dumb idea. He's most vulnerable when moving the body. Once he had it in his truck, he'd want to get rid of it PDQ. He wouldn't piss around cleaning up, and there were still mounds of empties around. But I can't stop thinking she was here somewhere. Otherwise, what was he doing that took two hours?" The second it's out of my mouth I regret asking that question, because my brain is flooded with images of him taking his time killing her. "Oh, God," I moan.

Kristy must have come to the same conclusion, as she utters a sound like a mewling kitten. After a bit, she suggests, "How about this? You pick the lock on the shed now, and if there's a kerosene heater and a mattress out there, we come back and check it out the next time someone goes missing. And we can get the aitch out of here now."

My surprise at her using a straight-laced old lady word for hell given how often she drops F-bombs is quickly replaced by the realization I'm anxious to leave, too. "Good idea," I reply.

Kristy hops off the table, landing with an odd, hollow-sounding thump. "Eek! The floor just wobbled. It doesn't feel safe. If this floor is rotten—"

"We better get out before it collapses under us," I say, finishing her sentence for her. "Next time, we'll come in daylight so we can have a better look and avoid rotten areas of the floor."

We hear a vehicle. Heavy footfalls on the back porch. The door swings open. A man steps inside. He shines his flashlight in our faces and says, "Ladies."

# Chapter 15

"Welcome," I say, and pull my duffle bag close. "But if you talked to the same guys we did and you thought this was a warm place to crash for the night, you got suckered just like we did." My heart pounds and I struggle to keep my voice calm. I'd like to throw in a relaxed chuckle, but I'm afraid it would come out as a squeak. "But you have a vehicle. You'd be better off sleeping in that. By the way, you got room for two more?"

He points the beam of the flashlight away from our faces, probably surprised that we're not trembling in fear and might actually have a reason to be here other than to vandalize the place. If we are trembling, it's not noticeable. I hope. Now that I'm not blinded by his flashlight, I get a good look at him. If thought he'd look amused, he doesn't.

"I own this place. You're trespassing," he says. "Didn't you see the signs?"

"Um, no. It's dark, and, um, well, maybe we did, but a guy we met told us other people stayed here."

"How did you get here?" he asks.

"Um, we walked."

"It's a long way from anywhere."

"Well, we got a ride as far as The Pioneer House," I say, and breathe out a long sigh. "That's where the guy we met works."

"Yeah. Colin," Kristy adds.

Colin? This is a detail she thinks she has to add? I hope my surprise doesn't register on my face.

"So, this Colin guy sent you here?" BBB asks.

"Yeah," I say. "Do you think we could stay?"

He shifts his weight from one foot to the other, apparently considering the merits of my story. Then his shoulders relax, and he says, "No. You can't stay. You'll freeze." He swings his flashlight around to illuminate the door. "Go on out," he says. "Wait in my truck where it's warm, and I'll give you a lift to the highway. You should be able to get a ride from there tonight."

"Okay," I say, and sigh again. "That's really nice of you. But could you drop us back at The Pioneer House? That guy—"

"Colin," Kristy says.

"Yeah, Colin. He said we could go home with him if we waited until he got off shift."

"So, why didn't you wait?"

"We didn't trust him," Kristy says.

"But you trust him now?"

"It's better than sleeping in a Goodwill collection bin," I say.

"Okay," Beer Belly Boy says, and gives us his big-toothed smile. "Now, go on out. I'll just need a couple minutes to nail the plywood back up."

I head out the door and down the steps, with Kristy following behind me. We climb in, pile our bags on the floor under out feet. Kristy sits in the middle and puts one leg on each side of the gearshift.

Although there's no chance he can hear us, I whisper, "Maybe you should keep both legs on this side of the gearshift so you can be ready to jump if I open the door."

"He seems nice. I think you're wrong about him."

When he's finished securing the plywood, he comes to the truck, slides into the driver's seat, and we start off. "Don't take this wrong, but you gals look a little long in the tooth to be hitchhiking," he says.

"It's, um, kind of an adventure. Something we'd never done. We both ended up unemployed, thought it would be a good time to take a little vacation. On the cheap, you know. But our money ran out sooner than we thought. Figured on getting a ride all the way home today, but only got as far as that restaurant. We were panhandling in the parking lot when they chased us off."

"Well, they were pretty nice about it," Kristy adds, and smiles prettily. I hope the smile isn't too much

"Fine. I'll drop you off at that restaurant, but if you don't trust this Colin guy, that restaurant is a lousy place to try and get a ride. You'd be better off at the Stockman's. At least it's on the highway. You'd likely get one of the regulars to give you a ride wherever you want to go," he assures us. "Maybe even all the way home. Where is home, by the way?"

"Calgary," I say, just as Kristy says, "Vancouver."

"Well, I live in Calgary, she lives in Vancouver," I explain.

He sniffs, clears his throat, rolls his window down, and hawks a loogie.

Before he can extoll the virtues of the Stockman's, I say, "Well, the guy at the Pioneer House—"

"Colin," Kristy says.

"Yeah, Colin. He said he'd be getting off at two-thirty and we could go home with him if we didn't get a ride before then. But aside from not trusting him, two-thirty? We want to be up and on the road first thing so we might as well stay up," Kristy says.

"So, you figured you'd just break into my house," BBB says.

"Yeah, well, I wanted to go to a truck stop," I say. "You know. See if we could hook up with a trucker—"

"Like a trucker would be better than Colin?" Kristy says and blows out a derisive *huh!*

"Anyhow," I continue, "we compromised, decided to go to, er, your house, and start out again early."

"But then it turned out the heat wasn't on like we were told it would be," Kristy says. "We are *so-o-o* lucky you came along."

I wonder why I don't gag. But thankfully, BBB appears to accept this much-too-complicated lie, clicks his tongue, and says, "I'll drop you off at the Husky." He turns on the radio set to CKSW 570—All Country, All Day—playing a song that's heavy on steel guitar.

Kristy says, "Hey! I like this song!" She starts humming along, throwing in the occasional words.

End of conversation.

When we're in the Husky lot, we thank him and bail out. As we hurry to the entrance, Kristy turns around to wave to the guy.

"For God's sake, Kristy!" I hiss.

Judging by the number of rigs in the lot, the restaurant is busy, and as we step inside, the truckers and oil patch workers look away from their meals long enough to gawk. Kristy smiles at everyone. Although she would be open to it, I need the toilet badly enough that I don't want to stop and chit chat with random men, so I herd her into the ladies' bathroom.

"Damn! I hate to think of how cold and tired we'll be now that we have a couple of miles to walk back to my truck," I say.

From the cubicle next to mine, Kristy says, "I'm sorry."

"For what?"

"For saying I didn't trust Colin."

"It was okay, but did you have to give him a name?"

"I just thought it made it more real. And why wouldn't we take him up on his offer? We needed a reason not to, or why would we go to BBB's shitting house?"

"Good point. But now we're a lot farther away from the truck than we would be if he left us at The Pioneer House. My fault.

I'm the idiot who mentioned we might get a ride with a trucker that gave him the idea to bring us here." I'm done, finish up, flush and go to the sink to wash my hands. Kristy is beside me at almost the same moment.

"For future reference, Kristy, the first rule of being a successful liar is to make it as close to the truth as possible, and the second rule is not to say too much. But you are definitely a gifted actress." I chuckle, and now even though we have a long, cold walk ahead of us, we have a laugh.

"So, you're not mad at me?"

"No."

"Good," she says. "BBB was decent, after all. He's not much to look at, but he was nice. He doesn't even have that big of a beer belly."

"You haven't seen him in a T-shirt."

"Well, it's no worse than half the rich guys in three piece suits I deliver drinks to at the Ranchmen's Club. He doesn't seem like a killer."

"What does a killer seem like?"

"I don't know, exactly. Just not like him."

"Serial killers are often very charming. It might've been a different story if I was there alone, or maybe we were just lucky his partner wasn't with him tonight."

"He has a partner?"

"Well, no. I mean, maybe. I've never seen anyone with him, other than his wife that one time."

"Do you think maybe K.C.'s right, and you've just let your, um, *imagination* run away with you?"

I bite my bottom lip, and with a sigh, admit, "I really don't know anymore."

She takes her jacket off, removes her pullover, stuffs it in her bag, puts her jacket back on, but doesn't zip it up. "Anyhow, we might not have to walk. Maybe we can get a ride at least as far back as The Pioneer House." She checks her look in the mirror and gives her breasts an upward nudge. Satisfied her scoop-neck T-shirt displays her cleavage to advantage, she smiles and says, "There!"

If we thought Trina was going to let bygones be bygones and invite Kristy into her house, even just to shower, we misjudged her ability to hold a grudge.

It's Monday morning. Kristy and I are at Jesse's for our secret meeting.

"I thought I'd be in like Flinn after that party," Kristy says. "We all had *such* a good time. I got along *so good* with her biker friends. You'd think she'd be happy about that, but from the looks she gave me, I don't think she liked it much at all. Mark thinks she's jealous. So, unless something changes, Mark's the only one welcome in her house. Which is okay, because if I did find her books, I wouldn't know what I was looking at anyway. He's the one who knows what to look for."

"True. So, has he been able to find anything?"

"Not yet. I'm telling you it's a good thing I got on at Billie's. The customers tip way better than the Bistro customers. Besides great tips, if it wasn't for having someplace to go, I'd be bored out of my mind. You know how small the lab is. Almost like living in a jail cell. You won't believe it, but I've been so bored I've started helping out with the barn chores."

"What? You? You're kidding!"

"Nope, not kidding. Imagine that! Me, shovelling shit! Well, that's not true. I don't shovel shit. But there's an orphan calf in the barn that's really cute. I like feeding her. That's my job, getting her formula ready and then bottle feeding her. I even brush her and take her for walks. I wish you could come and see her."

"I'm allowed to go in the barn, you know. It's not Trina territory. But you're right, it's not a good idea for me to go visit you. I'd sure love to see that, though: you in the barn, feeding a calf! Last time you lived here, I don't think you went into the barn more than once or twice, and now you're taking care of a calf?"

"I know! Crazy, huh? It's just, I've been thinking, Mark has been talking about getting his own place. Like, his own ranch, as big as Wacasko-Wâti, he says."

"Really?"

"Dreaming, right? But what if this thing with Mark is permanent? If he does get his own place, or even if his job at the Rocking R keeps on, like if Felix doesn't want to come back full time, will he want me if I'm not, um, more like you? Like, no makeup, no manicures, no monthly hair appointments?"

She's never been able to understand my lack of interest in those areas, so I don't take offence. "You really like him enough that you'd want to stay here with him?"

"I do. Crazy, huh? So, I have to learn how to do ranch stuff," she says, and gives her head a little shake. "It's awful, Lindy. I think he might not want me to stay. For the first time, I like a guy more than he likes me."

"Don't be silly, Kristy, I'm sure he likes you."

"He does. Just not enough. He's never said he loves me. He hasn't even asked me to be his girlfriend. Like that might make it too official. He introduced me to the hay delivery guy as Kristy. Not my girlfriend Kristy, just Kristy. Like I'm a ranch hand or something." An expression of misery crosses her face, then she laughs and says, "Anyway, I'm still working on him. That's why I'm taking care of the calf."

"He doesn't stand a chance," I tell her.

"That's right," she agrees. "Say, I meant to ask you, were you out on some P.I. assignment yesterday?"

"Yeah. Just for a couple hours in the afternoon. Why?"

"Remember that time we were surveilling K.C. and he went into Billie's, but only stayed a few minutes? Well, he came in yesterday and all he did was use the payphone."

"The payphone?"

"It's out in the vestibule, so I only saw him when someone came through the doors. But he must've been on the phone for ten minutes. Then he was just gone."

"Well, now it makes sense. He doesn't want that unlisted number to keep showing up on the phone bill."

"Yeah. But he must of knew I might see him on the phone, and that I'd tell you."

"I haven't told him or anyone else that you're working there or that I'm meeting you here. Not even Red. That way, there's no chance of anyone letting something slip. He knows we talk on the phone, but if he shows any interest at all, I just say there's no news."

"And Mark didn't tell him?"

"I guess not. Since Felix hired Jonesy, our guys don't work over there so they're not interacting with Mark much either. He still comes in for a cinnamon bun like before, but if K.C. doesn't know you work at Billie's, I guess Mark hasn't told him. They're not exactly close. It's like, unless K.C. has a job for him, he avoids him. And the fact is, since I know K.C. will lie to me, I don't trust him. We seldom talk about anything other than what TV show we're going to watch."

"I'm sorry, Lindy," Kristy says. "Is it because he wants kids? Would it help if you had a baby?"

"Have a baby now, when our relationship is in this sorry state? No thanks! I may be crazy, but not *that* crazy."

"What will you do?"

"Just ride it out, I guess. What else can I do?"

"Well, you could kick him out."

"Yes, I could. And don't think I haven't thought of it. But it's not like we fight or anything. We're just going separate ways together. And, he has an investment in Wacasko-Wâti. I don't have the resources to pay him out."

"An investment?"

"Yeah. His money built the indoor."

"And you put his name on the title or something? Is there something legal, you know, forcing you to pay him something?"

"No, but I want to do what's right. Besides, we've lived together long enough he's legally entitled to a share of the ranch and the business." I sigh and click my tongue. "I sure never thought it would come to this."

"I'm as pissed at him as you are," Kristy says. "I think I'll stick some gum in the coin slot, so he has to go somewhere else for his phone fuck."

# Chapter 16

Next morning, Mark has his usual coffee and a cinnamon bun, but I'm surprised to see he's at a window table instead of the staff table. I get a coffee and join him there.

"How come you're sitting over here?" I ask.

"Just thought I was too late, and everyone's already had their break. If I sat there, no chance anyone would join me."

"So, random customers join you often?"

"Er, no, but I guess it was more that I didn't want to sit and stare at the wall."

"Not much to see from here either, other than an empty parking lot and a pile of snow," I say. "You should've sat over by the fireplace so you could see the barn and the corrals, at least."

"Turns out it didn't matter where I sat, since you're joining me now." He removes his hat and sets it on the window ledge. "Kristy is pissed because I can come here but she can't, so I'll take a couple cinnamon buns to go, so she won't feel left out."

"You're very thoughtful," I say. "So, I hear she's feeding—" I'm cut off mid-sentence by the roar of a diesel engine. I turn in time to see an explosion of shattered cedar panelling at the entrance. The glass in the door and the nearest large window shatters, sending glass tinkling to the floor.

Mark and I jump to our feet and race to the door, but although we can see it's a truck that hopped the curb and hit the building, the door is wrecked, and we can't open it. We run to the wine-tasting room and exit through the patio doors there. Mark is faster than me, but neither of us gets around the corner in time to see more than the truck backing away.

"Hey!" I shout, "don't you dare drive away!"

Mark is nearly even with the back bumper when the driver floors it, spinning the wheels and spraying snow and gravel our way before he races out of the yard and onto the road.

Other than the entrance area being cordoned off, the wall temporarily closed in with plywood and plastic, and a sign on the sidewalk directing customers to access the Bistro through the patio doors in the wine tasting room, it's business as usual. The cops and insurance people have all been and gone. Now all we have to do is wait.

We moved the staff table to the farthest reaches of the wine tasting room to make up for the loss of space for regular customer tables thanks to the repair area. It has the added advantage of being more private. At present Stu, Red, K.C. and Mark are with me, enjoying a coffee break. Naturally we discuss the latest catastrophe.

"So, if we do the work ourselves, the insurance company will pay us?" Stu asks.

"That's right."

"How come SGI doesn't pay?" Mark asks.

"They will, but not up front. Our insurance company pays and then gets the money back from them. Thankfully they've waived our deductible, but it takes time, and we can't wait that long for the repairs to be made. As it is, the doors are a special order item and won't be here for weeks."

"Gerard says the truck was stolen," Red adds.

"Cops won't do anything anyway. And, of course, the dirty bastards stole a truck to do it. They wouldn't want to wreck one of their own. I hope they rot in hell! *Grrr!*" I growl. "Every time I think of it, my blood boils. I don't get mad often, but I swear, if I get the chance, I'll beat the living shit out of every last one of them!"

"Big tough Lindy," Mark says, and chuckles.

"You really think you don't get mad often?" K.C. says. "Seems to me you're mad a lot."

I glare at him and say, "I am not!" Although with him accusing me of it, I'm starting to get mad at him right now.

"Like you were going to beat the shit out of Bart, right?" Mark says.

"What do you mean?" I ask.

"When you confronted him that time at the Powwow. Practically had smoke coming out of your ears."

"Oh. That guy's name is Bart?" I ask. Then I think back. The Powwow incident was before the flood. "How do you know about that? It was before you came."

"Um, sure, but the guys still laugh about it. You know. Proud of how they got you wound up."

"Well, isn't that nice. I give them something to laugh about," I say, and add a snort. "Anyhow, more recent entertainment: I felt like punching his lights out when he made that remark about Rocky over at Felix's rodeo, too. And I'd bet dimes to donuts he's the one who shot the horse. There must be something the cops could arrest him for. I bet he's behind our latest catastrophe."

"You say you didn't see enough of the driver to make out who it was?" Stu asks. This is probably the tenth time he's asked that question.

"You just asked me that," I reply. Then I'm sorry for being sharp with him. In a softer tone, I say, "No, I saw him all right, but only for a second, and all I remember is that he was wearing a hat and sunglasses. And maybe had a little beard." I reach across the table and give his arm a rub, a sort of apology for snapping at him. My reaction was partly that I was already halfway fuming, thinking about the attack, and partly that Stu's forgetfulness is getting worse, and I worry he might have dementia.

"Oh," he says. Thankfully, he doesn't appear offended.

"I didn't get a good look at him either, Stu," Mark says. "All I could tell the cops was that it was a white Dodge one ton dually. Didn't get the whole plate number." This is also about the tenth time Mark has told Stu this. I'm grateful he's kinder to my old friend than I was.

"It was kind of funny, though. Mark damn near trampled me, trying to get out the patio door ahead of me," I say. "You know you have to wait until the door's open before you go through, right Mark?"

"Any excuse to grab you," Mark says. He grins. I look at K.C. He isn't grinning.

"Anyhow, it'll work out," Red says. "We move the door over so we can have a proper cashier desk there like we talked about, and the cash register can be moved off the pastry case. Some good will come of it."

"Trust you to come out with the glass half full view, Red. Main thing is, no one was hurt," I say, and sigh. "He chose the slowest time of the day, the lull between the early birds and the lunch rush, so there was no one in that area. Imagine if he did it when the seniors were on their way out."

Everyone agrees the timing was about as good as it could have been. And then I wonder if it was deliberate, and if so, how he knew. It's not like any of them ever hang around here to scope it out.

"Would have to happen so close to Christmas when we have parties booked. And when it's so damn cold! Going to cost a fortune to heat the place, what with that big, uninsulated section," I say. "On the weather side, too. There's already been some snow blown in."

"Why don't we put up some temporary insulation?" Mark suggests. "Stuff some in the cracks where the snow came in. Cover it with vapor barrier. Wouldn't look any worse than it does now, and you'll need the insulation anyway, so when the door arrives, take it down and re-use it. One bale should do it."

"Excellent idea," I reply. "Would you have time to go buy some and get that started today?"

"I would," Mark agrees.

"Good. I'll call Home Hardware and let them know you can put whatever you need on our account." I draw a deep breath and add, "Should we put bollards on the sidewalk all around the building so the assholes can't do it again?"

"Probably a good idea," K.C. says.

Great. Another expense we have to incur, thanks to Trina. It seems like we're always reacting instead of being proactive and taking the fight to her. So much for cutting the head off the snake.

I answer my office phone. It's Kristy. This is unusual. "Hey, girlfriend!" I say. "You have news that couldn't wait until our meeting Monday?"

"No, it can't wait, 'cause I'm totally freaked out, and I have to talk to someone," she replies. There's a catch in her voice as if she's on the verge of tears.

"Oh? Why? What's wrong?"

"Beer Belly Boy was at Billie's last night. Well, I think it was him, anyway. You know he's got those big teeth? He smiled at me."

"Don't all the men smile at you?"

"Well, sure, but it wasn't just the usual. I've been thinking about it all night. I think he recognized me."

"Really? You mean from when he caught us breaking in? How could he? You know, it was dark, and he didn't shine his flashlight on our faces for long. And since I was doing the talking, mostly my face. And we were wearing big clothes. And if I remember correctly, you had your hair tucked up into your toque. Plus, he wouldn't be expecting to see you at Billie's." I want to remind her this is at least an hour's drive from his usual watering hole and who goes that far out of their way for a beer? But there was that time I thought I saw his truck in the parking lot. And I've definitely seen it in town. Instead, I say, "So, supposing it was him. Was he with anyone?"

"Just some guys. I don't know who they are," she replies. Then she draws a quick breath and adds, "Lindy, I'm sure he recognized me, because he was all squinty-eyed, like he was trying to remember, and then he smiled." I hear her sigh. Then she says, "I don't think he seems nice anymore."

"We'll talk about it some more on Monday," I say. "Meanwhile, try not to worry."

<hr>

As it turns out, I don't see her on Monday, because on Sunday night, I'm awakened by an unusual sort of crackling or roaring sound. I don't open my eyes because it seems like part of my dream, and I don't want to wake up. But the noise is insistent, and there's light coming in around the curtains almost as if someone turned on the yard lights, but there's something wrong with them because they're flickering. Flickering? I open my eyes, jump out of bed and go to the window. There's smoke and flames coming out the window of the barn.

"K.C.!" I scream. "The barn's on fire!"

Usually slow to wake up, now he instantly sits bolt upright and asks, "What?"

I'm already pulling on sweatpants. I scream again, "The barn's on fire! I'll call 9-1-1! What horses are in tonight?" I know the answer: all the stalls are full. I only halfway hear his response as I'm pulling a T-shirt over my head while racing down the hallway to the telephone. "Barn fire at Wacasko-Wâti," I scream at the 911 operator. Then in answer to her question, I rattle off the address.

"I'm sending the fire department now," she tells me. "Stay on the line."

"I can't! We have to get the horses out!"

"Ma'am, don't—"

I slam the receiver down before she has a chance to tell me not to go in. That it's never safe to enter a burning building. I know that. But we have to at least try to get the horses out. K.C. is already in the porch pulling on his boots and jacket. I'm only slightly behind him as we race across the parking lot to the barn door.

K.C. slides the door partway open and is greeted by a blast of heat. "Looks like it's in the tack room," he says. "Can't go in this door. We'll have to go in the back way." He runs around the corner and down the side, with me right behind him. He slides the door open just wide enough for a horse to fit, and no wider. No use giving the fire more oxygen.

The horses are restless. Agitated. I struggle to remain calm, knowing I can't act panicky, or the already nervous horses will sense it and might refuse to leave their stalls. We hurry down the alleyway. K.C. grabs the horse closest to the flames. I get the next one haltered and pass the lead to K.C., then go to the one across the alleyway. I halter it, and consider getting another, but the one I have is so wild-eyed and spooky I'm not sure I could handle two. We lead the three of them out, staying as calm and quiet as possible despite the instinct to run. Even so, their heads are high and they're snorting. When I get out, I find the Pedersens waiting. I hand the rope for the horse I'm leading to Johnny. "Take him into the indoor. Tie him there and come back."

I race back to the open doorway. Having handed his horses off, K.C. is there ahead of me. Stu is here now, and follows K.C. in. I'm right behind him.

The fire has progressed alarmingly. The heat is intense and the smoke so black and thick it's nearly impossible to see any-thing despite the bright flames now engulfing the far end. It's a lucky thing we took the horses from the stalls across from the tack room first, because by the time we have three more horses out, that part of the barn is fully involved. I cough and pull my sweatshirt up over my mouth and nose and endure the stinging in my eyes as I go in again and settle for the closest horse. When I've got him out and handed off, I turn back and start through the door. K.C. grabs me. "Stop, Lindy!" he demands. "It's not safe! We won't be able to get the others."

"But Chica's still in there," I cry. "I have to get her!" I try to get out of K.C.'s grasp, but he just holds me tighter.

A horse screams. There's a loud crash as if something, maybe part of the hayloft, has collapsed.

"You can't save her, babe," K.C. says.

The fire department pours thousands of gallons of water on the fire, but it soon becomes obvious the best they can do is to save the nearby buildings. They continue to hose the flames, but turn half their hoses on the indoor arena and the Bistro as water tankers come and go. Despite the many thousands of gallons of water poured on everything, the heat is so intense the nearest corrugated PVC windows on the indoor are melted, some of the junipers in the landscaping go up like candles, and the fir beams of the pergola attached to the Bistro a hundred feet away are scorched. All we can do is watch while the barn is reduced to a pile of smoldering rubble.

We lost our hay, all our tack, half a dozen barn cats, and six horses, among them, the beautiful, sweet little mare I've loved since she came to live with me as a weanling. We're surrounded by neighbors and friends, all commiserating with us. I spot Mark in the crowd, but it seems he's just there and then gone. When I can't take any more condolences, I go up to my house, fall on my bed, and try to stop replaying images of Chica, her terror and her awful death. I hope the fire chief was right when he said she would have died from smoke inhalation and wasn't burned to death. I cry until my throat aches and I can't cry any more.

When K.C. comes and sits on the bed next to me, I'm not ready for company. I say, "Go away."

"Babe—"

"Don't you *dare* say she didn't burn to death, or that you're so very sorry, or that I can always get another horse," I warn. "I don't want another horse! There'll never be another one like Ch-Chi—" I bury my face in the pillow and sob with renewed vigor.

He rubs my back until I'm calm, then says, "Lindy—"

"What? Why don't you go away and leave me alone?"

"Well, this is important. You know Mark was here, but Kristy wasn't?"

I did notice it, but with everything going on, hadn't really paid attention. Now her absence strikes me. With the smoke visible for miles, so many neighbors, Mark included, came, but not Kristy? "Um, yeah?"

"She didn't come home last night, Lindy. No one has seen her since she left work."

I worried about the Bistro burning and it turns out it's the barn that should've had sprinklers, but I never would have dreamed Trina's crew could be so evil as to burn a barn full of horses. But as evil as that is, it's nothing compared to what I fear is happening to my friend. I draw a sharp breath as my body convulses in a shudder.

# Chapter 17

I t will take days for the rubble to be safe for access by the fire cause determination team the insurance company is sending. We can't start clean-up, not even to find Chica and the other horses' bodies so they can be buried.

Long before the firefighters leave the scene, the cops interview every Wacasko-Wâti employee, including seasonal field workers. It's my job to call everyone in for their interview. It helps get my mind off the hell I'm living in. When all the employees have been called, I get in the shower and stand under it until the water runs cold. Getting cleaned up and back into my usual jeans and T-shirt feels good.

What doesn't feel good is seeing a strange vehicle pull up to my house, right up until it's nearly touching the garage door. If it's another reporter, I think I'll scream. But the man who gets out isn't a reporter. He's a friend. Kristy's husband Jim. Of course, he has to be here. The significant other is always a prime suspect. I go to greet him, and he pulls me into a hug. With a sob, he says, "Lindy, how could this happen? It's that man, isn't it?"

"No, Jim. There's been a few..." I was going to say Kristy is just one woman in a string, but he's bound to have heard of the women who were missing *and murdered*, so I stop there. "Everyone's down in the Bistro. We have the tasting room cordoned off for interviews. You'll be staying with us, of course. Unless you want to get settled first, come with me. Since you're ex RCMP, maybe Deputy Coltrane will actually listen to you."

"Deputy?"

"Well, actually he's a sergeant. Non-Commissioned Officer in Charge, in fact. I just call him Deputy Coltrane because he reminds me of the character in Dukes of Hazzard. Just about as competent," I explain. Together we walk down to join the others. We're down to a core group of Wacasko-Wâti and Rocking R people, Sgt. Coleman and Cst. Gerard. I introduce him to everyone.

Sgt. Coleman says, "Have you got a minute, Mr. Spears? We need a statement from you."

"Of course," Jim says. "I brought a photo. Thought you'd want that."

"Sure," Sgt. Coleman says.

The two head off to the more private area, but rejoin the group in the main area maybe ten minutes later. Once we're all together, I start discussion by claiming Trina's crew started fire.

"You also blamed them for flooding your blueberry field and shooting a horse, without evidence," Sgt. Coleman says.

It's on the tip of my tongue to tell him blueberries don't survive here, but saskatoons even grow wild, and in my opinion, taste better, but then he's new to Saskatchewan, so I think better of it. I'd like to remind him that I think they're behind the sewer backup and planting the rat that got us shut down, but all those things fade in importance next to Kristy being abducted, so instead I tell Sgt. Coleman about Beer Belly Boy and my belief he took Kristy.

"And why do you think that?"

Okay, how to summarize. "Because SGI suspected him of insurance fraud. Exaggerating his injury. I was surveilling him for them and followed him to this old house he claimed he'd had to stop renovating because of his injury. I was hoping to get video of him working on it. I didn't, but he went there every day. Why? There was no sign he was doing anything in there. And I found a ticket to a grunge band concert in the garage. I know BBB, er, Mr. Asselstine, is a country music fan. Can't see him traveling to Minot for a grunge band concert, can you? Did the last woman, the one that was just found murdered, go to it maybe?"

He ignores my question and instead, asks, "So, you were inside the house? The garage?"

"Er, yes."

"They weren't locked?"

"Well, the garage was, but the house wasn't. At least the back door wasn't." It's a technicality, but I don't elaborate, because he's giving me a squinty-eyed look as if I had somehow done something wrong. Maybe he missed the point.

"Anyway, he, er, caught Kristy and me there a couple weeks ago, and Kristy told me just the other day that he'd been in Billie's and she was worried he had recognized her."

Rosco doesn't respond. When Kristy told me about it, I gave her all those reasons why he wasn't there or if he was, he wouldn't recognize her, so I guess he's discounting that for all the same reasons. I can't blame him. There's so much I want to say, but he's not interested.

We meet other volunteers and organize search groups at Billie's, where Kristy's little red Fiero was found. Once the bushes, pasture and ravines within body-dragging distance of Billie's turn up nothing, the searchers go home. I can't blame them. It's cold and getting dark.

Over my objections, Red insists on opening the Bistro for business tomorrow.

"We're going to take a hit on our cash flow as it is," she says. "Will you call our staff back in for tomorrow morning, or do I have to do it?"

"I'll do it." Anything to get my mind off what's happening to my friend.

We underestimated the number of customers who thought seeing a smoldering pile of blackened rubble was worth a drive out to the country. The morbid curiosity of people who flock to see a train wreck I guess. The Bistro is so busy there are people waiting for a table. I pitch in to help.

"Some special guys who are super stars at determining where the fire started and what caused it have to do their thing first," I tell those who ask when it's going to be cleaned up. Honestly, I've explained this so many times I sound like a stuck record. I think we should put up a sign over the coffee bar that says yes, we lost some horses, and no, we don't know how long it will take to rebuild. I'm really tired of talking about it. It's impossible to keep my thoughts from Chica's last moments when well-meaning folks keep reminding me. Is it ridiculous to mourn an animal so intensely?

That Kristy is missing has been on the news and there's lots of talk about it. A few of today's customers know she worked here not long ago. Of course, they feel a need to mention it to me. I'd rather they didn't, but they mean well. When I've rushed to the back for a private moment to compose myself about a dozen times, I decide to call in a couple of servers I laid off just a few weeks ago to take my place, so I can stay home.

The message light on my answerphone is blinking. It's K.C. explaining he'll be away until early January. I didn't even notice him leaving. Jim was in the house when K.C. packed up and left, but didn't mention it because he thought I knew. So we sit and share carafe after carafe of coffee, and I imagine my face is as long as Jim's. It's preferable to being subjected to everyone being so nice.

Once the Bistro closes, we go back down. Jim joins the Wacasko-Wâti/Rocking R people while I go into the kitchen to help Red finish closing up for the night and tell her K.C. has gone.

"Gone where?" she asks.

"He didn't say, other than he hasn't got the kids' Christmas presents yet."

"He doesn't have to stay away for weeks. He could get their gifts and drop them off, then come home," Red mutters.

Despite feeling the same way, I find myself defending K.C. "He said one more searcher wouldn't make a difference. Nothing to keep him here, since, um, you know, we're down a couple lesson horses and he had already booked off all his lessons over Christmas plus he has a clinic to do in Pillerton so he might as well go straight to that after Christmas. Right?" I tell myself to quit running off at the mouth like that and take a breath now and then, because I sound as if I'm trying to convince myself.

"Yeah, right. No use staying here to have Christmas with us," Red agrees, then mutters, "and maybe to be there for you. I mean, what with things..."

"Well, you know his kids were supposed to spend a couple days here at Thanksgiving and that didn't work out. Now there'd be nothing for them to do here, so they canceled again. It makes sense for him to go and spend Christmas with them there," I say.

"We got other horses and an indoor ring for them to ride in," Red says. "Always some excuse. How come we ain't even so much as laid eyes on them kids despite him living here all this time?"

"They're allergic to horses."

Red utters a dismissive snort. "How would they know that? Ever been near a horse?"

"Of course, when they were little. You know K.C. had horses then. And if one of them had an asthma attack, how long would it take us to get them to the hospital? At least in Regina they're only minutes away."

"Sure. And where's he staying?" She looks as me, narrow-eyed, and I know she's thinking the same thing I am.

"Anyhow," I say, "that's unimportant. We're done here. Let's join the others."

Since Jim and I came in, Mark, Dwight, and Cst. Gerard arrived. The cheerful crackling of the fire, the Christmassy-pine scent of the nearby tree, the cheerful, brightly-colored Christmas lights are incompatible with the prevailing mood. I turn the lights off, but there's nothing I can do about the crackling or pine scent.

Earlier, I called Sgt. Coleman for an update. He sent Gerard. He's next to Mark and across the table from me. "Sergeant Coleman couldn't make it?" I ask Gerard as I slide onto a chair across from him.

"He's, er, curling in the bonspiel in Pillerton this weekend," Gerard explains, and studies the label on his beer bottle.

Not that there's anything wrong with Gerard, but doesn't a high-priority missing person case warrant the attention of the man at the top? Not if there's a bonspiel, apparently, and not if he can send a constable, even if it's one whose shift ended hours ago.

Jim is between Dwight and me, and I'm not sure because I can't see his face, but I suspect he hasn't quit glaring at Mark since he came in. Or maybe ever.

"Okay, so, what are you doing about finding Kristy?"

"We're on top of it, Lindy," Cst. Gerard assures me.

"Doing what?"

"Well, we've interviewed Billie's staff, and we're in process of running down as many customers as possible from that night."

"Have you got names, like, of customers?"

"Um, not all, of course," he admits. "The regulars were pretty straightforward. Anyone who ran a credit card, too."

"A lot of that business must be cash," Red says. "And if someone picks up the tab for other folks and pays with a credit card, no way of knowing who all he was paying for."

"True," Cst. Gerard says.

"What about security cameras?" I ask.

"There's one at the cash register, but it's grainy and blurry. Not much use as far as identifying anyone."

It's on the tip of my tongue to criticize Billie's security camera, but ours is about the same. When our door got crashed, we were barely able to make out the plate number. Instead I say, "I guess most people pay their server anyway. Maybe I could look at the tapes, though. I've seen him often enough I might I recognize him even if the tape is grainy."

"Cops said we should stay out of it," Stu reminds me.

"Well, I'm not satisfied with that. Remember what Felix said when Janey was missing? They keep telling us missing persons is a top priority, but they're not doing anything."

"We are, though. Doing something," Cst. Gerard insists.

"But Rosco completely ignored me when I told him about Beer Belly Boy."

Me using a slur against his boss causes Cst. Gerard to squirm. I'm not sure if it's because he doesn't like it, or maybe he's struggling not to laugh. In any case, he responds, "No, he didn't ignore you, Lindy. He had members from the Swift Current Detachment check that house out right after you mentioned it."

"Really?" I can hardly believe it. Rosco did police work? And in a timely manner? "Are you sure they checked everything?"

"He told me to assure you we're all trained and experienced, and, er..."

I imagine the rest of what Rosco told him to say was *and you're not*. That takes the wind out of my sails, but only temporarily. "Um, okay, good. Could I see the list of that night's customers, Constable?" I ask. "See if any of the names pop?"

"I'd have to ask," he replies.

"But probably not. Privacy issues and so on."

"Probably not," he admits.

"Well, someone paying their bill in a pub doesn't have an expectation of privacy. It would make sense for me to have a look at the video, right? I'm the only one who knows what he looks like."

"Like I said, I'll have to ask," Cst. Gerard replies. He looks around the table and says, "So, if that's it, folks, I'd like to get home in time to tuck my daughter in. I'll keep you posted." He gets to his feet.

Dwight pushes his chair back and as he gets up, says, "I'll walk out with you." The two men take their leave.

"You done, darlin'?" Stu asks Red.

"Just need to finish up," she replies.

"Nothing that can't wait until morning, Red," I tell her.

"You sure?" she asks.

"Of course, I'm sure. I'll give the kitchen another look before I lock up."

"Okay," she agrees, and leaves with Stu.

"I promised Kristy's family I'd keep them posted. They'll be waiting for my call. I should go up and phone them now," Jim says.

"You go ahead," I agree. "I have a few things to do, but I won't be far behind you." Despite what I just told Jim, I don't plan on going to my house for hours. I've just been waiting for everyone to leave. But Mark shows no sign of going anywhere. I putz around putting things away and turning off lights, but he doesn't take the hint. Maybe he can't bear the thought of going to that cold, dark little room. Here I am, focused on my own fear and worry, while his must be exponentially worse. He's taking his time finishing his beer. I get myself a glass of milk and sit with him.

"Not tired yet, Lindy?" he asks.

"Sure, I'm tired. Exhausted, really, just like you. But being tired doesn't mean I'll be able to sleep."

"Yeah. I know what you mean," he says, and sighs. "That place is just not the same without her."

Looks like he's settled in for the night. To move things along, I offer, "How about I get you a scotch to go with what's left of your beer? To help you sleep."

"Um, sure, that would be great."

When I've poured his drink and set it in front of him, I take my seat again and say, "Honestly, I don't know why Deputy Coltrane doesn't pay more attention to my suspicion about Beer Belly Boy."

"He said they checked it out."

"Yeah, and their searching skills are no doubt much better than mine, since they're trained and experienced. Asshole," I say, and finish my milk. "You know, when BBB caught us in his shack, Kristy and I had just decided that we would go back again when another woman had been snatched, to see if the heat was on then. Never dreamed it would be Kristy that was snatched, or that it would be me, on my own, looking for her."

"Let's hope the list of Billie's customers turns up a lead. Or the surveillance video. Other than that, they're probably working on other leads."

"I hope so."

"But you doubt it."

"Let's just say I only halfway believe it. There's good people in the Detachment, but they'd be farther ahead if Coleman stayed out of it and let them run it. There's a reason I call him Deputy Rosco P. Coltrane."

"You think he's inept."

"An ass-kisser promoted to his level of incompetence. He's a big part of the reason Felix didn't sign on for another tour."

"Well, he's what we've got. He says we have to stay out of it. What else can we do?" Mark shoots his scotch, then studies my face and says, "You're not going to stay out of it, are you?"

"No. I'm not going to let another hour go by sitting on my hands doing nothing while Kristy is suffering. Where is she? At best she's alone and scared. At worst... Well. With nowhere else to start, at least, I'm going to Dogpatch as soon as you finish your beer."

He says, "Lindy, don't be crazy. It's late. Tomorrow is another day. And, if you're right and the guy, what do you call him? BBB? If he's the killer and you go poking around in his territory, you could run into him and then he'd have you, too. It's not safe."

"I'll be careful."

He utters a long sigh and says, "Well, if you're determined to do this, I guess I better go with you."

# Chapter 18

It hasn't snowed much since Kristy was kidnapped, so it's no surprise there are plenty of vehicle tracks, but they all end at the front porch of BBB's project house. From there on, nothing but pristine, unmarked snow in the headlights. The van isn't good in snow. I only chose it because my truck was low on gas, and I wasn't sure I'd find a gas station that was open all night. Faced with this, I hope it wasn't a mistake. I slow to a crawl as I edge into the snow, unsure how deep it is and with only a general idea of where the road is.

Mark asks, "Where are you going?"

"I usually park behind the bushes in the back lane," I explain.

"Why?"

"So my van's out of sight. You know, to make a getaway in case he comes along."

"Lindy, he's not going to 'come along' now. Not at this time of night."

"You were the one who told me it wasn't safe to come here, and now you think I'm being too careful? It was dark and long after his dinner time the night he caught Kristy and me here."

"But not after midnight, am I right?"

"Yeah," I agree.

"It's more likely you'll get stuck in the snowbank than be caught again. Turn in there and park where he's obviously been parking."

"Yeah, and if he shows up?"

"I'd take care of him."

"Okay, Mister Big Stuff. But my Glock's in the glove box. Hand it to me, would you?"

"You have a Glock?" He opens the glove box and gets it out. "Jesus, Lindy! Do you know how to use this? Do you even have a permit for it? To have it in your vehicle?"

"I took lessons when I first got it. About the permit, I'm not sure, um..."

"Are you really prepared to shoot him? You'd go to jail."

"No, I wouldn't. He's got my friend in there somewhere. It would be justified."

"You don't know that, and besides, he'd more likely get the gun away from you and use it on you. I'll take it."

"You don't think he could take it from you? Just because you're a guy?"

"That, and I've got firearms experience. Gun club member for years. Plus, I know jujitsu and fifteen other Japanese words," he says.

"Very funny," I say.

"Just park in front."

Mark's probably right. No need to hide my van in the lane. I pull the van right up to the front steps.

"At least this proves he's been coming here," I say. "Why, in this cold? Something's fishy."

"Well, you did say he was renovating."

"I said he was *pretending* to renovate." I turn off the engine and we get out. "Grab the toolkit, please, Mark." He slides the door open wide enough to reach it, and we hoof it through nearly knee-deep snow around to the back. I dig the hammer out of the toolkit and start prying the plywood off. Mark takes it from me and does the job, pulling it open far enough for us to get inside.

"So much for it being warm in here," Mark says.

It's not as warm as I had hoped, but it's not as cold as the last time I was here, either. "It's warm," I insist. We shine our flashlights on the walls, floor and ceiling as we move through the kitchen, living room, both bedrooms. I had hoped a closer examination would reveal a false wall somewhere. A room that seemed smaller inside than the outer walls would suggest. Nothing.

"Same as last time?" Mark asks.

"I guess so," I reply, and sigh. "I was so sure."

"So, nothing to see here," Mark says. "Let's go home."

I'm about to admit defeat and follow him to the door, when I realize the table was in the middle of the room when Kristy and I were here, and now it's back in the corner like when Felix and I came. "That's it! The table!"

"That's what?"

"I think the table is right on top of the part of the floor that sounded funny when Kristy hopped down off the table onto it. Why would he move it? Maybe it's hiding something."

"Lindy, you think there's something under the floor? Didn't you say there's no basement?"

"Yeah. Maybe not a basement, but there could be a crawlspace. And a lot of these old houses had a root cellar, or a coal cellar, under the house. Maybe there's a trap door." I pull the table away from the wall. "I could kick myself for not thinking of it sooner. Get the other end, would you?"

Mark is moving maddingly slowly, but I guess I can give him a pass on that because he doesn't have my imagination, and he's not as fired up as I am. But he comes and takes the end, and we shift the table to the opposite side of the kitchen. I hunch over and train my flashlight on the floor where it had been, and there, up against the wall, I find two hinges, rusted enough to match the floor. There's a seam in the wood surrounding a section of floor, four feet square. On the side opposite the hinges, a handle, inset so it's flush with the floor. With the trap door fitted so tightly the seam looks no different than the joins in the floorboards and with a table leg covering the handle, the trap door is next to invisible.

"Mark! Look at this!" My heart pounds. I grasp the handle and try to lift up, but can't budge it. "It's stuck."

"It's probably nothing," Mark says. "Hasn't been opened in so long it's stuck."

"You don't know that. Give me a hand."

He nudges me out of the way and gives the handle a half-hearted tug. "Nope. Stuck solid."

"Come on, big strong *I'll take the Glock* guy, you're not even trying." I take another try, and this time the door lifts. It's surprisingly thick and heavy. Even open only a few inches, I can feel a flow of warm air.

"This is where the heat's coming from!"

He grasps the edge of the door and tips it back against the wall. I shine my flashlight beam down into the hole and call out, "Kristy?"

"Lindy!" she screams, as her face pops into view. She cries, "Oh, my God! It's you!" She dissolves into tears. "I thought it was that buh-buh-buh-bastard!"

"Mark's here too! You're safe now. Come up. I'll help you."

"Can't." She holds up her arm to display the steel cuff on her wrist. "This is as far as I can go."

"We'll get that off," I say, and shine my light on the steep, narrow steps. More of a ladder, really. I want to hurry, but me falling won't help anyone. "Mark, shine your flashlight on the ladder while I go down." I shove my flashlight into my sleeve, turn and hold the ladder as I take the steps carefully until I'm at the bottom. I'm standing on the thin mattress that covers the floor of the small room almost completely. Kristy launches and hugs me, sobbing.

"Oh, my God, Lindy! I was afraid you wouldn't come.

"You should've known I would, silly," I tell her, give her a return squeeze.

"I gave up hope when I heard someone thumping around upstairs and I screamed my head off, but they left."

"Yeah, that was likely the cops. Those most excellent searchers that Rosco thinks are more skilled than me. In fairness, it took me a few tries to find the trap door, too, as you know. Anyway, let's see what we have to do to get you free." The chain is attached by a bracket screwed to the top of the wall. I can't quite reach it. Mark probably can, though.

She holds her wrist out to show me the steel bracelet secured in place by a padlock. "Can you pick it?" she asks.

"In the time it would take me to pick it, we can undo the other end of the chain and have you out of here," I tell her. I call out, "What's keeping you, Mark? I need a screwdriver. There's one in the toolbox."

His face appears overhead, but instead of starting down the ladder, he puts one foot on it and slumps down to sit on the edge of the opening. "I'm not coming down," he says.

"The steps are wobbly, but I'm sure they'll support you," I say. "I can't reach the bracket holding the chain, but I think you can."

"I'm not worried about the steps being wobbly. I don't need to come down, because you're going to stay and keep Kristy company."

He can't be serious. "What? That's not funny. Come on, Mark, quit fooling around."

"I'm not fooling around, Lindy."

Kristy wails. A buzzing of disbelief fills my brain.

"You just had to keep sticking your nose in, didn't you, Lindy?"

A storm of jumbled thoughts fills my head, making it impossible to speak. I can't undo Kristy right now, but I have to get out. Can I get past him? I have to try. If I act fast and surprise him, I think I only need to get up a couple of steps to reach the opening, put my hands on the floor and vault up and out. I launch myself at the ladder, turn and leap. I manage to get my hands over the edge and onto the floor, but before I can hoist the rest of my body up to get a leg out, he raps my fingers with the butt of the Glock.

"Uh, uh, uh!" Mark says. "Try that again and it'll be your pretty face I use this on instead of your hand."

"Ow!" I howl as I drop down and stumble a few steps backwards before I get my feet under me. He hurt me! The fact that Mark, my friend, is involved in kidnapping, is shocking enough, but that he would really, deliberately hurt me is almost beyond belief. I draw a deep breath, and pieces of the puzzle start to come together. Finally, I rein in my runaway thoughts enough to ask, "The truck crashing into the Bistro. That was you, wasn't it?"

"It was."

"So, that was why you didn't sit at the staff table."

"Right. My hat on the window ledge was the signal that there were no people in the way. We didn't want to hurt anyone. We're not monsters."

"Only a monster would kill Janey and that other woman."

"That was Alfie's thing. He's been busy with that for years. It wasn't until he had this, um, holding cell dug that he started keeping them. Took him a while to get it dug. Had to haul the dirt away bucket by bucket. Not an easy job, as you can imagine."

"Yeah. Hard work being a murderer," I agree. "So, that time BBB caught Kristy and me here, you called him to tell him we were coming, didn't you?"

"Of course. Otherwise, he wouldn't have come here so late. By the way, that was some story you came up with, about the bartender. We had a chuckle at him dumping you so far from where you really wanted to go. But we only wanted Kristy. Otherwise, you would've gone in the hole then."

"Why are you doing this? What do you want?"

"Why, Wacasko-Wâti, of course. Figured you'd sign over the ranch to get her back, and all we'd have to do would be to threaten to kill a couple of kids if you ever told anyone. Maybe Trina's. You seem to be getting pretty attached to him. Although it would be easier to get one of the teenagers. But now you've thrown a kibosh into that plan. You're a problem and I don't know what we're going to do about it."

"Mark, you can't get away with this. Kristy going missing is one thing, but how are you going to explain my disappearance? Everyone knows you were the last person to see me."

"That's what I mean. You're a problem. I could say I left when you told Red you would close. I agreed to meet up with you first thing in the morning and went home. I had no idea you were going anywhere. But that doesn't get the ranch signed over to us. Like I said, you're a problem."

I draw and exhale a long breath. "I guess you know Russ Benson."

"I do. Met him through the club back in Ontario. One of our members was in the Pen, and Russ was always bragging about his businesses and complaining that he needed someone to look after them. With my accounting and business degrees, plus my willingness to, er, *bruise* the occasional federal statute if necessary, I was a perfect fit. It was a bonus that I knew you from university. Wouldn't have come to this if Trina hadn't been bugging him to change his will. Why would he leave anything to her? She was just some Bimbo he fucked a few times."

"He didn't have to marry her," I point out.

"He didn't marry her. They weren't even a couple. Did you know there are women crazy to get with prisoners? Even the serial killers? In fact, he's really popular. As for Trina, who knows if the kid is even his? But it could be, so killing him was never really an option. Russ agreed to let Trina live in his house and he'd pay child support. No skin off his nose. Then he hears the kid is with Red and Stu more than with Trina. What's he paying child support for? So she can party on his dime? So, he sent me to see what was going on. But more than that, Russ is horny to get some fracking leases, and that stupid old fuck Stu won't even listen. Yammers about it causing earthquakes, contaminating wells, gas coming out of the faucets, blah blah blah. Why stop with the Rocking R? We get both properties, and we'll drill, baby drill! Nice steady income for doing nothing. And me here permanently to manage his businesses." He chuckles. "Told you I was going to get property, Kristy. Didn't believe me, did you?"

"Did you have to burn down our barn?" I ask. "You know we had horses die in that fire."

"That wasn't us. Why would we destroy an asset?" Mark stands up and grasps the edge of the trap door, ready to close it. "Well, this has been fun. But I need to get a few miles away from here to dump your van before daylight, Lindy, so I gotta go. *Sayonora*, ladies."

"Mark!" Kristy screams, "Don't go! I love you!"

The trap door crashes down, cutting off any reply he might have made. Scraping sounds overhead. Mark is shoving the table back on top of the trap door.

Kristy slumps to the mattress, back against the wall. My legs aren't steady, either, so I sit beside her. I expect her to erupt into fresh wails, but she just slowly shakes her head and says, "I told you he didn't love me."

That's what she's thinking about right now? Sometimes she's so smart, and other times she comes out with the strangest stuff. The way her mind works is bewildering.

"At least they won't kill us," Kristy continues. "They'll have to let you out to sign the transfer, you know, giving them your ranch, and then they'll let me out, too. I know you love that ranch, but you lived in town before. That bank you worked at in Katawasis Lake said you could be assistant manager again. And the ranch has had so many problems, would it be so bad not to have to deal with all that—"

"Jesus, Kristy! They're not going to let us out. Not ever. We know who they are. They'd be looking at a life sentence." I don't add that their only recourse now is to kill both of us and forget getting the ranch. That was only going to work as long as they were anonymous. The instant I found the trap door, our fates were sealed.

"But we'll promise not to tell the cops," Kristy insists.

"Do you think they'll believe us, even if we pinky promise? They're not that stupid."

My harsh tone starts her crying again. I can't blame her. It's brand new to me, but this has been a longer, terrifying ordeal for her.

In a softer tone, I say, "Don't cry, Kristy. We'll find a way to get out of here. We're Katawasis Girls. We can do it." I get up and start examining every part of the little room. The ceiling has insulation stuffed between the floor joists. Two walls are concrete, likely the corner of the foundation, but the other two are just dirt. Hard packed, and we have no tools, but still, digging out is a possibility. If we have time.

I climb the ladder far enough to push on the trap door with my back. The ladder wobbles, but the door doesn't budge. "I don't think I'll be able to open this, especially not with the table on in. Might have to wait for a chance when the Beer Belly *Bastard* opens it. *If* he opens it."

"He has to come down to refill the kerosene heater," Kristy replies. "He brings a bag of stuff. Usually, a sandwich or two and a banana. Bottle of water."

"That's if they want to keep us alive. I imagine Mark has to check in with Russ for instructions, and that might give us a day or two. So, we might have all day to dig out, or he might come first thing in the morning now that he's got a new, er, guest."

"How would digging out help? It wouldn't get you outside. You'd still be trapped in the crawlspace, and I'd still be chained up. You'd have to leave me behind. You wouldn't do that, would you? Leave me behind?"

"Of course, not," I lie. Better one of us out than both of us trapped. At least then I could bring help.

I notice a rock embedded in the dirt wall near the shit bucket. "If we can dig this rock out, we'd have a weapon. Maybe there's more, so we could each have one, and hit him over the head when he comes down. He wouldn't be expecting it. Then I could go up, get his screwdriver, and—"

"Are you kidding? He's a big guy and I'm not tall enough to reach his head. I'd only be able to hit him in the belly, or maybe in the balls, and no way is he going to let me do that. I thought I might stab him in the back when he's going up the ladder, but I can't reach that far chained up like this, and besides, the biggest blade on my Swiss Army knife is barely two inches long so it wouldn't kill him and might make him mad enough to—"

"Oh, my God, Kristy! You have your knife? He didn't take it away?"

"No. He only checked my pockets."

"And he wouldn't expect you to be armed and dangerous," I say. "So, the blade might not be long, but there's other things on the knife. Such as a screwdriver. Let's have a look."

She pulls the knife out of her shirt and lifts the chain over her head to hand it to me. There's a surprising number of tools even on these small models. In addition to the two-inch blade, this one has two different bottle openers, corkscrew, nail file, even a tiny pair of scissors, but most importantly, a screwdriver. "Great! Now I just need something to stand on so I can reach that bracket."

The only items at hand are the shit bucket and the kerosene heater. The bucket would be best, but it would have to be upended and with no out-of-the way place to dump it, it's a poor second choice. The heater it is. I move it into position and carefully step up, one foot on each side of the handle. Not a great step stool at the best of times, now it's wobbly thanks to the lumpy mattress it's on.

"Can you shine the flashlight up here for me, Kristy? And while you're at it, steady the heater so it doesn't tip."

It's while I'm unscrewing the third screw that the light flickers. This is no time for the batteries to die. Some Katawasis Girl I am. I not only let Mark talk me out of my gun, but I don't have my own Swiss Army knife, and I left without checking to make sure I had fresh batteries in my flashlight. Kristy doesn't say anything so I don't point it out. I manage to get that screw out and I'm working frantically on the fourth when the flashlight quits. The screwdriver disengages from the screw and in the dark, no way can I get it back in to finish the job. Is one screw, partly removed, enough to hold it in place?

I put a hand on Kristy's shoulder and carefully step off the heater. "Okay, give it a tug." Nothing happens. "Here. Maybe our combined weight will do it."

Kristy shrieks with delight when the last screw lets go and the chain crashes to the ground. I think I shrieked, too.

We sit huddled together. In a few minutes my eyes have adjusted to the dark, and I realize there's enough light from the heater that I'm not completely blind. I stand, feel my way to where I remember seeing that protruding rock, and run my hand along until I feel it. I start scratching.

"What are you doing?" Kristy asks.

"I'm going to get the rock. That way, one of us can stab him and the other can knock him senseless. Not necessarily in that order."

She comes up beside me and says, "I'll do that. You look for another one."

"You're going to ruin your manicure," I warn.

"Now you're a comedian? At least I have fingernails, which makes me a better digger."

I step away, but my foot bumps against the ladder. I lose my balance and as I'm stumbling, catch the first thing my hand closes around: one of the rungs about halfway up the ladder. It moves in my hand. This isn't surprising, because the whole thing is rickety, but it actually seems loose. It rotates when I twist my wrist.

"Get that rock out, Kristy."

"I'm working on it," she replies.

"Well hurry up. I need it."

"What for?"

"Well, this one rung is loose. I think there must only be one nail or screw or whatever, attaching it to the rail. I need the rock to pound it—"

"You're going to fix it?"

"Yes. But not the way you might think."

# Chapter 19

The hours in the dark hole crawl by. I alternate between sitting with my back against the wall, lying down, and feeling my way along the walls for anything I might have missed. Nothing. We go over our plan again and again. I think we both doze off now and then. When the heater runs out of fuel, what little light it gave off is gone. Being in absolute darkness is worse than I ever imagined it could be, and it's surprising how quickly the temperature begins to drop.

"No one's going to come," Kristy says into the void. "They're going to let us die a long, slow death." Her tone is surprisingly flat, as if she's saying out loud what she's been thinking for a while and accepts it.

"Don't think like that, Kris. We have to believe someone will come for us."

"Who? Who else besides me and you knows about this place?"

"Well, K.C., of course. And Felix."

"But they don't know about the trap door."

"No, but they'll come. I'll get on the ladder and pound on the trap door, and they'll be able to hear that. They'll find it. Don't worry."

I hope I sound confident. Felix is a thousand miles away. Until he calls home, even his family doesn't know where he is. I don't have contact info for K.C.'s ex, so there's no way for Red or Stu to let him know I've been taken. The cops can probably find him, and I guess they'd want to talk to him, significant others being prime suspects after all, but how long will that take? Will they track him down before Russ makes the only decision he can make, and gives the order to kill us?

I decide against telling Kristy these things. No use both of us knowing she's right about our chances for rescue.

I've slipped into an exhausted slumber when I'm awakened by sounds of movement up above.

"Kristy!" I hiss, "he's here! Get ready!"

We both scramble to get up, and as nearly as we can tell in the complete absence of light, take our places. We hear the table legs scrape the floor overhead. Slowly the trap door is raised and light pours in.

We can't see him from where we're standing pressed against the wall out of the beam from the flashlight, but he can't see us, either. Kristy said he always shines the light down first, then sets the flashlight on the floor at the edge of the opening so he can use both hands to grasp the ladder as he climbs down. We're prepared for this. There's a rattle and a length of chain drops down. He's brought what he needs to chain me up, too.

The first foot appears on the top rung. He places his other foot on the same rung as the first. That's odd. BBB wears red boots?

He puts his right foot down on the second rung and reaches his left foot to the third. The one I had pounded the nail out of and then friction-fitted back in place. It seems like slow motion. I'm holding my breath. When he shifts his weight onto it, for a split second I think it's going to hold. Then the rung breaks away. Everything seems to happen at once. Something hits my nose. BBB crashes down, landing on the mattress with a *whump,* and utters a long groan. Kristy and I both leap across the mattress to stand over him, Kristy at his head with the rock raised, and me beside her, ready to stab him in the, well, whatever, when he utters a loud, very feminine-sounding cry. Neither of us follows through with our attack. I hop up onto the bottom rung of the ladder, grab the flashlight, and swing it around to bear on the fallen person.

"Oh, my God!" Kristy shrieks, "it's a woman!"

"Mrs. Asselstine," I say.

"You know her?" Kristy asks.

"Sort of."

"She's rescuing us?"

"Not intentionally." I focus the beam of the flashlight on her face.

The woman turns her face to me and moans, "I think my arm's broken." She tries to move, but yelps in pain and collapses back.

I turn the beam of the flashlight on her arm. It's definitely bent where it shouldn't be. "Yup, I'd say so. How's your head? You're lucky you hit the dirt wall instead of a concrete one, but you might still have a neck injury or a concussion."

"*Ahhh!* My shoulder! It really hurts. Help me up," she cries, and sobs loudly.

"Us? Oh, we can't help you."

"But I can't move! My leg! *Gaaahh*! I hurts too. I'm too hurt to even move."

"Then don't move."

"I need an ambulance."

"I'm sure your Alfie can help you with that, when he gets here."

"But he's not coming until tomorrow," she sobs.

"At least he's not going to leave you here. Come on, Kristy, up the ladder and let's get out of here."

"Should I still knock her over the head?" Kristy asks.

"Don't hurt me! Please don't hurt me!" Mrs. Asselstine begs. "I came to rescue you! I'm sorry for what my husband did."

"Right," I say. I swing the beam of the flashlight around until it illuminates the can at my feet. "That's what you brought the chain and the bear spray for, to rescue us? Sure, Kristy. Go ahead and hit her, if you want to."

Kristy thinks about it for a few seconds, then shrugs and drops the rock before gathering the chain and starting up the ladder.

"Looks like neither of us is a psychopath, so you're luckier than your victims," I tell Mrs. Asselstine. I push the flashlight into my sleeve with the business end pointing out and put the knife in my pocket. As satisfying as it would be to stab her, just once, for Janey, now that she's incapacitated and it's no longer the heat of battle, I can't bring myself to do it. But nothing's stopping me from emptying the shit bucket on her head. She's coughing and sputtering as I climb out of the hole and drop the trap door.

We race out of the kitchen, through the living room, and out the front door. Mrs. Asselstine's old Duster is parked nose up to the front porch. I'm halfway down the steps when it hits me: did she take the keys and lock it? Are the keys in her pocket?

Kristy goes to the passenger door while I take the driver's side sending up a silent prayer as I try the door. Hallelujah! It opens. I slide in while Kristy gets into the passenger seat. The keys are in the ignition. I give the gas one pump and turn the key.

It grumbles, but doesn't start.

I pump the gas and turn the key again. Still nothing.

"Hurry up!" Kristy says.

"I can't hurry up."

"Give it more gas."

"Have to be careful not to flood it," I say, but give it another little pump and turn the key. It starts. "Yes!" I exclaim. And then the engine stalls. No amount of pumping or turning the key starts it again. I push the accelerator to the floor and hold it for a ten count while cranking the engine over. No luck.

"Oh, my God," Kristy exclaims, and points back toward town. "Someone's coming! Maybe it's someone looking for us."

"It's BBB's truck."

"Try turning the key again!"

"We don't have time to mess with this. We have to run."

We both jump out of the car and scurry around to the far side of the house. "Damn! I left the flashlight in the car. With luck he didn't see us," I say.

Kristy says, "Slow down!"

"Can't," I insist, and take her hand to pull her along. We're in calf-deep snow that hasn't been walked or driven on. Her legs are shorter than mine and she's wearing her silly spike-heeled so-called snow boots that are just barely ankle high. She's been on short rations for days so her energy levels must be low. She's struggling.

There's enough moonlight to see the shed. When we're behind it and out of sight from the road, I let go of Kristy's hand and stop.

"You okay?" I ask.

"Yeah," she says, although the way she's gasping for air, it's obvious she's not. "It's tough going, though."

"I know. But it won't take him long to find his wife alone in the hole, Kristy."

"That liar! She said he wasn't coming back until tomorrow. And she said she came to rescue us."

"Yeah. Lies," I agree.

"What a stinker, eh? Especially after you dumped the bucket on her!" She giggles, and I'm once again bewildered at how her mind works. I guess it is worth a chuckle.

"Anyway, we have to hustle, at least until we get to where he can't drive," I insist. "We don't have to go far, but we have to stay off the roads, because if we go where he can drive, he'll catch us. In fact, he might not have to stay on the roads, because his truck is a four by four. The train tracks are that way." I point across the unmarked snow of the open area to the train tracks. "There's a fence cordoning off the railway right of way that will stop him, though, and from there, it's only a few blocks to the Pioneer House."

"Aren't there houses there? Can't we just go to the first house that has lights on?"

"By God, you're right. So. Ready?"

"Ready," she replies.

We head out into the open. It's no more than a few hundred yards to the right-of-way, but with the snow so deep and the near panic in my heart, it seems much longer. Kristy falls a couple of times, so I take her hand again. We reach the fence. If it was barb wire, we could go through it, but it's page wire with a single run of barb wire on top. We can't go through it. We have to go over it. I'm at a post starting to climb when the beam of a searchlight sweeps over us, stops, and comes back. I turn and see the truck leave the road and start plowing through the snow, heading our way. No pit lamping deer or a horse now, he pit lamped us.

"Damn him!" I mutter. I hold the post with my left hand and climb the wire just high enough to get my right leg over, then turn, switch hands on the post, swing my other leg over, and hop down. I sink in the snow past my knees. "Here, Kristy, I'll help you." How I'm going to help her, I have no idea. I guess just by holding the chain so it doesn't tangle in the wire.

She seems to have stalled out, maybe trying to figure out how to get over a fence that's taller than she is and dragging the three-foot length of chain.

"Grab the post, hand me the chain, and climb," I tell her.

The truck engine roars. Can I hope he's stuck? Apparently, he is, as the truck rocks back and forth, then catches and is plowing its way through the snow in our direction again. Kristy looks back and sees it, utters a scream, and scurries up the fence. As she's over and jumping down, her jacket snags on the barb wire. Now she's hanging on the fence. I try to work it loose, but it's right through the fabric at the hem and won't rip, even with her full weight on it and me tugging at it besides.

"You're going to have to take it off, Kristy."

She struggles to unzip it, but the zipper seems stuck. The truck is mere yards away when the zipper lets go and she falls in a heap beside me, half buried in the snow. This may be the first time she's ever regretted wearing such a skimpy t-shirt. I grab her arm and pull it and the chain out of the jacket's sleeve, help her up, and take her hand. "Okay now, up the bank."

"But you said we'd be safe on this side of the fence," she complains.

"I might have been wrong about that," I say. "He can climb the fence, too."

"I don't think I can go any further."

"You have to, Kristy. You can..."

At that moment, the engine roars again and the truck hurtles into the fence. The wire screams as the truck pushes into it. It stretches but holds. Kristy shrieks. Maybe I do too. He backs away as if getting ready to take another run at it. In this cold, the wire is brittle. I'm surprised it held this time. I doubt it will withstand a second hit. At best, he'll get out and chase us. And he might be able to drive right up and over the tracks.

"Kristy, he's going to make it through. He'll run us down. Come on!" We definitely need more distance between us before I'll feel safe enough to slow down.

"He must be really mad," Kristy says.

"Yeah. Really," I agree.

The earthworks, while not high, are very steep. We scramble up on all fours onto to the train tracks. Just like in Dogpatch, a street runs parallel to the fence, but unlike Dogpatch, there are inhabited houses on the far side of it. We half run, half slide down the embankment to the fence, and make it over without catching any clothes or body parts on the wire just before we hear the truck engine roar again. There's a screeching sound, then *zing!* as the wires break. More growling engine noise and the front end of the truck pops into view on the earthworks. Another roar. The truck leaps up onto the tracks.

"I don't believe it," I mutter, "how did he manage that?" As astonishing as it is that he not only broke through the fence, but also made it up onto the tracks, now it seems he's unable to go farther. He's spinning the wheels, blasting gravel and snow out behind, then stops. The truck is quiet. Or as quiet as an idling diesel can be.

"He's getting out!" Kristy shrieks.

The truck door swings open. BBB slides out and starts down the embankment toward us. He can't toss us into the truck, not with it stuck up on the tracks a hundred feet away and on the other side of the fence. What does he think he'll accomplish if he catches up with us? Neither of us wants to hang around to find out. We run.

People have come out of their houses to investigate the noise. The nearest man hurries to us and asks, "What's going on?"

"He had us locked up," I say. "That man that's chasing us had us locked up!"

"Oh, my God! Okay, my wife's calling the cops. You'd better come in," he says. He turns and yells to the other bystanders, "The cops are coming. Tell them we have those women they've been looking for."

As he herds us up the steps and in the door, we hear sirens in the distance. A woman joins us, and says, "You must be freezing! I'll be right back." She scurries away down the hall, returns with a blanket and a pair of slippers. She drops the slippers at Kristy's feet and as she wraps the blanket around her, says, "Put these on."

Only now do I realize Kristy is missing a boot. "What happened to your other boot?" I ask.

"Lost it in the snow. I hope I can find it. These are my faves."

She kept going without complaint, even minus a boot, and after the ordeal she's been through, she's worried about a boot. I tear up, and even though I'm not a hugger, I give her a squeeze.

When I release her, Kristy turns to the woman and says, "Thank you." Now her teeth begin to chatter.

"I'm Emma, and that's my husband, Brian," she says.

"Don't worry," Brian says, "if that bastard makes it this far before the cops come, he's not going to get by me." He lifts the baseball bat from beside the door as if to punctuate his words.

Kristy and I introduce ourselves and follow her to the front room.

"I didn't hear a thing," Emma tells us. "We were downstairs watching a movie. Brian thought he heard someone with car trouble and went to take a look."

"He's got car trouble, all right," Brian says, and checks his watch. "The 8:10 to Calgary will be coming along PDQ. That gives him, oh, about five minutes to get his truck off the tracks."

"I don't think he can do it in time," I say.

"I don't think so either," Brian agrees, and goes to the front window to look out. Kristy, Emma and I join him.

Sirens intensify as RCMP cruisers converge on the house. Beer Belly Boy has just reached the fence when he stops and scans the cruisers coming this way, blue and red lights flashing, as well as the growing number of bystanders. He turns and scrambles back to his truck.

"He doesn't know about the train," I say.

"He's going to find out pretty quick," Brian says, and points at a single headlight on the tracks to the east. "Right on schedule."

It's coming fast. Now blasts from the train whistle join the sirens.

The engine roars. The truck rocks back, then forward, then back, but can't make it all the way up onto the earthworks or back down, either.

"Must be high centered," Brian says. "The tracks aren't made for cross traffic. Dumb thing to try. If he doesn't bail now, he's not going to make it."

As if he heard what Brian said, BBB jumps out and takes long, leaping strides down the earthworks, running for the fence as best he can in the deep snow. The train whistle is one solid blast now. Its wheels, locked in a futile attempt to stop, screech along the rails, sending out cascades of sparks that live on the snow for a heartbeat before disappearing. The locomotive smashes into the truck, shearing it in half. The engine compartment and most of the cab is in jagged pieces, propelled through the air along the right of way. The hood catches the fleeing man. His head flies off in a spray of blood before disappearing under the snow. His headless body stands for a fraction of a second before collapsing. The train continues down the tracks, slowing and finally coming to a stop a hundred yards farther on.

"Oh, my God!" Emma exclaims.

As much as I think it couldn't happen to a nicer guy, this is one of those visions that will haunt me for a long time.

Kristy says, "You know, he would've been better off running the other way."

# Chapter 20

Mid-morning Christmas Eve. Newton, still in his zip-up fleece sleepers, is busy moving all the Tupperware out of the drawer and onto the floor. Kristy, Jim, my mother Marie, Mom's husband Reggie, and I linger around the island, enjoying after breakfast coffee and Bailey's while planning our day.

"I hope you took the turkey out of the freezer yesterday, Lindy. How big is it? I think we should get it in the oven pretty quick."

"It's a fresh turkey the Hutterites delivered yesterday, Mom. I don't know for sure how big it is. Probably at least twenty pounds. Big enough to have lots of leftovers. Red's on top of it. Relax."

I hear a vehicle in my driveway. I get up, and careful to step around various lids and containers, go to look out the window. "Huh! It's K.C.," I say, and return to my seat.

"Thought he wasn't coming back until after the New Year," Jim says.

"That's what I thought." I mentally add, *maybe not even then*.

"So, better late than never?" Kristy asks. "I still think he's an asshole. Even if the cops didn't find him right away, he couldn't miss the news about you being kidnapped. He should have been back here before now. I don't even want to see him."

"Come on, sweetie," Jim says, "at least he's home for Christmas. Maybe he's got a good explanation for why he left when he did."

"What possible explanation would that be, Jim?" Mom asks. She and Reggie have been here since I was reported missing. They're staying until after Christmas, when they will head for Mexico in their motorhome.

Jim's only reply is a shrug.

Kristy says, "Maybe he heard the insurance company is settling the claim for the barn fire and will be sending Lindy a nice fat check."

"That's harsh, sweetie," Jim says.

I have to admit that's the first thing that popped into my mind, but then, he couldn't know about it. Or could he?

"Not harsh enough," Kristy insists.

The door swings open, and with a rush of cold air, K.C. steps into the kitchen. When he sees it's not just me here, a flicker of annoyance crosses his face. In a second, it's replaced with a smile.

"Hey, hello everyone," he says. "Marie. Reggie. Thought that must be your new Winnebago in the driveway. When did you guys get here?"

"We came as soon as we were notified that Lindy was missing, because we care about her," Mom replies.

"You know, I didn't find out she was missing until she was already home," K.C. says. He comes to where I'm sitting, leans in to plant a quick kiss on my temple, and asks, "Newt's here again?"

"Trina packed up and left with the bikers when Mark got arrested," I tell him. "No idea where she went or when she's coming back. I share babysitting with Red and Stu."

"Oh, okay," K.C. says. "Good. There's still coffee." He gets a mug out of the cupboard.

"I reckon there's things I need to take care of out in the bus," Reggie says, and gets up. "Coming, darlin'?"

Mom frowns, then says, "I guess so." She gets up, puts her mug in the dishwasher, gives me a knowing look, and follows him outside.

"Um, Kristy, isn't it time for your shift in the Bistro?" Jim asks. "I wouldn't mind a cinnamon bun."

"No, Jim, it's not time for my shift, as you very well know, and I'm not leaving," Kristy replies. She turns to K.C. and says, "I'm as pissed at you as Lindy is, K.C.! You buggered off and left it to everyone else to search for me? If you hadn't of done that, you'd of been here, Mark wouldn't have grabbed Lindy and you would've gone to Dogpatch with her and rescued me. It's because of you we went through all that... all that..." She chokes up and is unable to complete her thought.

"I'm sorry, Kristy. I really am," he assures her. "But some good came out of it, right? Otherwise, no one would've known that the killer's wife was his partner. Or about Mark's involvement. And if Mark cuts a deal—flips on Russ—maybe gives them all the info about his finances so they can seize the cash even better."

"What?! We were abused and terrorized, but it's okay because some good came out of it?" Kristy sputters.

"It's over, sweetie. You're okay. Everyone's okay," Jim says, and takes her hand. He looks at K.C. and says, "I think you better quit before you dig yourself into a deeper hole, buddy."

"Kristy, I said I'm sorry," K.C. says. "I was wrong to go. I realize that now. What can I do to make it up to you?"

"Nothing! Not a damn thing! I don't want nothing to do with you until Lindy forgives you. Maybe not even then." Kristy abruptly stands and says, "On second thought, Jim, let's go get a cinnamon bun. I can't stand being near him." She heads for the door without waiting to see if Jim is following.

Jim looks at me, shrugs, gets up and says, "Okay, guys, She Who Must Be Obeyed has spoken." He leaves, closing the door behind him.

"She Who Must Be Obeyed?" K.C. chuckles. "That's a good one. I think it applies to you more than to Kristy."

"It's not original," I snarl. If he wanted my forgiveness, he's off to a bad start.

"I'm sorry, babe," K.C. says. "I, er, I mean, can you forgive me? I know I shouldn't have gone. It was just that everything was in such a turmoil around here, I thought maybe one less person in the mix... and there was nothing for me to do, not really. Not with the school horses gone, along with all our tack. The boys and Stu can easily look after the stock here and at the Rocking R, and you don't need me to run the Bistro, so I just thought it made sense."

"Sure. And tell me, where were you staying?"

"Well, you know, I stayed with my kids."

"You mean with your ex."

"I, um, yeah. She's going through a rough time right now, so it was good for me to be there, you know, to help with the boys."

"A rough time?"

"Her husband left her and she's not coping. She's not strong like you are, Lindy. I knew you could manage without me, but she's barely getting out of bed. Didn't even have the Christmas tree up. I had to get the kids off to school, get meals ready, all stuff she couldn't do."

"Her husband? How did she remarry without giving you a divorce?"

"Well, not her actual, legal husband. The guy she was living with." He looks away and then back, continuing, "I was only there for the kids. That's all it was. I didn't sleep with her, if that's what you're thinking. Honest. I wouldn't do that. It's you I love."

"Yeah. You love me so much you bugger off without a word."

"I didn't plan to stay. I just went to drop off the Christmas presents, and that's when I found out how bad things were. I phoned and left you a message."

"And it's okay because you left a message? You called when you knew I wouldn't be in my office so that you wouldn't have to talk to me."

"No, I—"

"You took the coward's way out. You knew I wouldn't have accepted your lame excuses for why you had to be away for weeks. Bad enough any time, but over Christmas and New Year's? And when I'm already dealing with the fire, and my best friend missing? You didn't think I could use some emotional support?"

"I know. It was just better not to make an issue of it, I figured. Not with everything, like you say, so... Anyway, I'm sorry, and I'm back now."

"Um hmm." I study his face. He looks sincere. He reaches across to stroke my arm and smiles again. He seems to take my silence as acceptance, gets up and comes to put his arms around me. He strokes my hair and says, "I love you, Lindy. I understand why you're mad. I'll do whatever it takes to earn your forgiveness."

I'd like to believe him. I want to believe him. Then I remember all those phone calls over the past couple of months and how easily he can lie. I can't believe this was a spur of the moment thing.

He releases me and says, "By the way, any movement on the insurance claim?"

And there it is. The real reason he's here.

"Yes. The official cause on the report was accidental, believed electrical. The old microwave shorted out."

"Oh, great! So, we're in the clear."

"Yes. The adjuster dropped off a bunch of forms to list contents on. I'll give you some for your tack. You need to include the values. He said to get a quote from a tack shop for that."

"Is there a limit?"

"Yes, but I think it's enough."

There's a shriek from Newt. I jump up and go to him. He's pushed the drawer in and got his finger stuck. I pull his weight off the drawer and pick him up. There's a nasty dent in his finger that will leave a bruise. I cuddle him and kiss finger and his tears. K.C. barely notices. I can almost see the wheels turning in his head.

"Here, sweetie, you're okay now," I say to Newt, "Let's get Gaff." I carry him to the box of toys in the corner, set him down on the floor, and together we dig through to pull out the rubber giraffe. Newt promptly starts chewing on it and has forgotten about his finger.

"I'll get started on my list as soon as I bring my stuff in," K.C. says. "I already have most of it written down. I'll have to go over it again to make sure I haven't forgotten anything." For the first time since he got here, he looks genuinely happy as he heads for the door. He stops and turns back to ask, "How soon do you think I'll get a check?"

"No idea," I reply. We got together just when K.C. was losing his place in Katawasis Lake. He had no prospects and no other place to go. Was Wacasko-Wâti the real attraction?

"K.C., wait," I say.

He turns to face me and asks, "What?"

"You know you could've just phoned me to find out the status of the insurance claim. Don't worry, I won't cheat you out of your share."

"I didn't think—"

"There will be documents to be signed before any checks come. If you get your list back to me, I'll take it from here. Leave your ex's phone number. I'll call you when there's something for you to sign."

"My ex? Well, um, her phone number? Don't you have it?"

"You know I don't. You've always made sure of that. We were planning Christmas without you, and I don't see a reason for us to change that now. Don't bother bringing your stuff in. You're not staying."

Christmas isn't the sad event I half expected it to be. I guess K. C.'s right. His ex falls apart along with her marriage, while I'm so strong I'm not even bothered by my relationship ending. Maybe it's different because we weren't married, or maybe because it's been such a long time coming, but I'm not that strong, really, it's just that I cowboy up. A couple of times throughout the festivities I feel a stab of sadness and wonder where K.C. went, but I quickly push those thoughts out of my head. It helps a lot that I have my people around. Even Felix, who came home when Mark was arrested. He had no plans to be home for Christmas, but seems pretty happy that he is.

Our ranks are swelled by the addition of the girls Charlie and Johnny invited. It's a reminder they're not the little brown boys in their underwear who were playing in the dirt when I met them. They're young men now. Handsome, strong, responsible young men with girlfriends. Life goes on.

We closed the Bistro at three, so we have the place to ourselves and plenty of room for everyone. After dinner we have our gift exchange. Our family has always opened all our gifts on Christmas Eve, but with such a mix of unrelated people, this year everyone brought one unisex gift to put under the tree. One person at a time chooses a gift, or they can 'steal' one of the open gifts. Once they open their own gift it's too late to steal, so it's a bit of a crap shoot to trade it off. A Dwight Yokum CD changes hands twice before ending up with Reggie.

Gift exchange done, Reggie hauls out his guitar and we gather around the tree for a sing-song. He plays Ghost Riders in the Sky at least three times, and everyone joins in the yipie-aye-yays enthusiastically. It takes me back to the summer I met Red and Reggie, and my first love, on the rodeo tour, singing that song around the campfire every night.

He also responds to requests and plays all the usual Christmas standards before putting the guitar down. Then Charlie tunes the stereo to a country station and turns up the volume. We push the tables out of the way to make room for dancing. Little Newt's gregarious personality is starting to show. He crawls and toddles his way around to visit everyone. He manages to stay awake long past his usual bedtime, but when I give him a bottle and snuggle him into my coat on the floor in the corner, he falls asleep despite the commotion going on around him.

It's midnight when the boys leave to take the girls home, and the rest of us go to our beds. I know I'm going to regret switching from wine to rye and ginger ale. I lost track of how many I had. I stagger a little as I'm carrying Newt across the snowy parking lot and up to the house. Jim takes my arm to steady me. I give myself a mental reprimand for being so irresponsible when I have the baby to look after. Self-medicating?

Maybe I'm not strong, after all.

# Chapter 21

I've got Newt on my hip as I stroll down to check the progress of the construction project. Who doesn't like to watch shirtless men slaving away in the hot sun, muscles rippling under skins glistening with sweat? I have an excuse. Red sent me to tell the crew she's got lemonade ready and burgers on the grill. It's time for a lunch break.

It's six months since the old barn burned down and K.C. left. I think of him less and less, maybe because Felix being around fills the void he left behind. He's living in the big house on the Rocking R and has plenty to do looking after his own ranch, semen sales and the rough stock business, but spends as much time here as he does at his own place. I tell myself I'm crazy. He's seven years younger than I am and has his pick of buckle bunnies at every rodeo and all the single girls in town, so why does he seem so, well, so interested in me? I don't quite know what, if anything, I should do about it, so although he's quit calling me Auntie and we go to rodeos and dances together, I keep him at arm's length and ignore the gossip about the two of us. I have to admit his attention is flattering, though.

K.C. was arrested trying to buy Hillbilly Heroin, the street name for the oxycodone he became addicted to, from an undercover cop. I felt sorry for him. Then in the negotiations for the quit claim he had to sign before I'd pay him off, it came out he had a sizeable bank account funded by his fake alimony payments. His ex divorced him and remarried years ago. No wonder he never wanted his kid to spend time at the ranch. They'd be bound to mention their stepfather. Any pity I felt was short lived. Just one more kick in the teeth that made me wish I'd never met him. At the time, I was coming out of a bad relationship and had sworn off men. Kristy was constantly trying to set me up with guys she met at the pub she worked at. I told her I wasn't interested. Then I met K.C. when I boarded Chica at his barn and let my guard down. My suspicious nature wasn't suspicious enough. I was conned. Never again. Never *ever* again.

This morning, Felix is working with the crew that's framing our new barn. It's nothing like the old one, just a lean-to on the east wall of the arena building. After paying K.C. there wasn't enough money for a barn the size of our old one, but we'll have ten stalls, store our hay in the barn at the Rocking R, and bring over what we need a pickup load at a time.

Stu's senior's moments have rapidly become worse and more frequent. He's been diagnosed with early onset dementia, probably a result of his many concussions. He's no longer capable of looking after Newt, so when Red's working at the Bistro, I have him. What a treasure he is! I've discovered a mother instinct I didn't think I had. I'm plagued with the constant worry Trina will come back, and I'll lose him. I've talked to Jesse, and he is working to get me sole custody. I'm a blood relative, his maternal grandmother lives close by and would be prominent in his life and as Mark said, part of the reason he came here was that Russ didn't trust Trina to look after him. So, it's a definite possibility.

South Saskatchewan Fracking has offered a decent price for the ranch. I'm not seriously considering it. Kristy, who is back with Jim, can't understand why I don't jump at SSF's offer given all the problems I've had with Wacasko-Wâti. She wants me to move to town. I tell her I just got a new horse, but I think the real reason is the blood bond with the land that Trina spoke of. I can't imagine leaving. Whether I stay or leave, I guess I'll be the last Larsen on the ranch.

# CHECK OUT THESE OTHER GREAT READS FROM ROWAN PROSE:

Gayle Siebert has penned dozens of short stories, novellas, and novels for readers of all ages. They always feature strong female protagonists, and you can usually find a horse or two. Naturally, there has to be a good-looking cowboy somewhere. She was born in Saskatchewan, grew up in Alberta, and has lived her adult life in British Columbia. After more than thirty years as an insurance adjuster, she retired to her small horse farm, Idyllbeck, on Vancouver Island.